ALSO BY H.E. BATES

THE YELLOW MEADS
OF ASPHODEL

by

H. E. BATES

London
MICHAEL JOSEPH

CENTRAL

First published in Great Britain by
MICHAEL JOSEPH LTD
52 Bedford Square, London, WC1B 3EF
AUGUST 1976
SECOND IMPRESSION OCTOBER 1976

ISBN 0 7181 1499 X

554953

*Printed in Great Britain by
Hollen Street Press Ltd at Slough
and bound by Dorstel Press at Harlow*

The Proposal

'GREAT Heavens! What a mountain of raspberries! What *am* I to do with them all?'

At frequent intervals on summer mornings Miss Shuttleworth, coming downstairs in her ballooning magenta dressing gown to open her kitchen door in order to take in her milk bottle, try to assess what sort of day it was going to be and, most important of all, to say a series of affectionate hulloes and good mornings and God-bless-yous to the wrens, robins, chaffinches, sparrows and other small birds waiting on the lawn outside for the first crumbs of the day, would find on her doorstep a little gift: a basket of early strawberries, a dish of nectarines, a cantaloupe melon, a bunch or two of asparagus. She never quite knew what next would be there.

On the particular morning when she found on her doorstep a basket of ten or twelve pounds of the fattest, ripest red raspberries she observed also a thrush, its speckled breast almost white, gazing with intent longing at the basket of berries as if in anticipation of a fine fat feast.

'Now off you go. Don't be greedy. You know I don't feed you all till later. Then if you're good I'll bring you sandwiches. Tomato, cucumber, cheese, anchovy and, if you're very, very good, Gentlemen's Relish. But you must be patient. The day is young.'

As the thrush finally flew away to settle on the lawn beside the little stream that ran through the garden, there to cock its head to one side in the act of listening for a worm, Miss Shuttleworth lifted the basket of raspberries and took it into the kitchen.

The mystery of who brought these constant and unsolicited gifts to her doorstep had long remained unsolved. No note ever accompanied them. Then after some weeks of summer it began to occur to her that their arrival was invariably succeeded by the figure of a grey-haired middle aged gentleman in a brown and white tweed suit, not at all unlike the breast of the thrush, walking slowly past her garden gate, walking-stick in hand, and as slowly back again.

Often Miss Shuttleworth on these occasions would be engaged in trimming her yew hedge, the edges of her grass verge or hoeing weeds from the path that led to her garden. At such moments she would offer the gentleman in tweeds a greeting.

'Good morning, Professor Plumley. Nice morning.'

'Good morning, Miss Shuttleworth. Yes, a nice day. A day to remember.'

Miss Shuttleworth, more often that not dressed in a large scarlet straw hat and what appeared to be a floppy pink nightgown, would pause with her garden shears opened in the form of an executional cross and sharply remind the Professor that you could hardly remember something that hadn't yet happened.

'Ah yes, but it obviously will be.'

At such a point Miss Shuttleworth would remind the Professor that if there was anything either reliable or obvious about the English weather she had yet to hear of it.

'Ah yes, but I put it simply as a matter of optimistic conjecture.'

Damn silly remark, Miss Shuttleworth would tell herself, closing her shears with an executionary snap.

On the morning of the arrival of the large basket of raspberries Miss Shuttleworth, instead of snapping her shears, suddenly lifted her head sharply and said:

'Oh! hark at that blackbird. If ever there was a voice with all Heaven in it it's surely that one.'

'Oh! curse the blackbirds.'

Miss Shuttleworth, whose love of birds placed them far nearer Heaven and the Almighty than most human beings she knew, simply stared at the Professor with eyes that had in them ice, steel and pity in about equal proportions.

'Professor Plumley, are you aware of what you've just said?'

'Of course. I was merely cursing those damnable birds.'

'There are no such things as damnable birds.'

'In my garden there are. The wretched creatures eat all my raspberries.'

'*All* your raspberries?'

The Professor now looked acutely embarrassed. He pounded the ferrule of his walking-stick into the gravel path almost as if endeavouring to dig a hole in which to hide or bury himself.

'What I meant was that I have to be up at dawn in order to get any for myself.'

Miss Shuttleworth now found herself to be both enlightened and touched.

'Then is it you I have to thank for the gift of them this morning?'

'I fear so.'

Miss Shuttleworth, offering no comment on what she considered to be a remark of exceptional inanity from one who had been a university Professor of philosophy, simply smiled and said:

'Well, thank you. Thank you very much.'

'Not at all.'

'It's most kind of you. The only thing is that there are so many of them I simply can't think what to do with them all.'

'I thought perhaps you might make jam with them.'

Miss Shuttleworth at once informed the Professor that she had no great partiality for jam, especially raspberry.

The Professor confessed that she surprised him. He himself adored raspberry jam. It reminded him of the nursery teas of his childhood. He had also loved it on hot toast at his rooms in Cambridge. And what, if she didn't make jam of them, was she going to do?

Miss Shuttleworth, one of whose more absorbing hobbies was to make home-made wine and even brandies of a particular potency, said she thought of making a spot of wine with them.

'Wine? But isn't that rather sacrilege?'

Now how on earth, Miss Shuttleworth silently asked

herself, could making wine from the fruits of the earth be sacrilege? You might just as well maintain that it was sacrilege to make marmalade or rhubarb tart or horse-radish sauce or something.

Miss Shuttleworth, however, decided to ignore what seemed to her to be yet another highly unphilosophical remark and simply said:

'Then I suppose it's you I have to thank for the straw-berries and nectarines and melons and so on?'

Again the Professor could only express himself in three extremely painful words.

'I fear so.'

'Well, in that case, – oh, what time is it?'

The Professor took a gold hunter from his waistcoat pocket, consulted it and said that according to his calculations it was half past eleven.

Miss Shuttleworth, ignoring the fact that it was the watch and not the Professor who made the calculations, said:

'Good. In that case I think it's a good moment to go in and have a soupçon of something – or what nowadays they call a snifter.'

Politely the Professor thanked her all the same but said he was afraid he never partook of anything in the middle of the day. A modicum of sherry in the evening perhaps, but—

'Oh! Nonsense. Fiddlesticks. Come in and try a glass of one of my home-mades. It's the least I can do to thank you for all those lovely gifts.'

'Well—'

'Come along do, come along.'

The Professor, looking rather more like a shy lamb going to the slaughter than a retired Professor trying to enact the part of the country gentleman, followed Miss Shuttleworth into her cottage. There, in her inglenooked sitting room, Miss Shuttleworth proceeded to recite a list of the various liquid refreshments she had to offer.

'Red currant. Elderberry. White currant. Potato. Lemon. Orange. Blackberry. Elderflower.'

'Well, I hardly know. What do you yourself usually partake of?'

'Well, I'll tell you. If it's a damn cold morning I often start with a couple of pipe-openers of parsnip. And if it's a damn cold night I finish up with a good whack of cherry brandy. My own seven year old.' Miss Shuttleworth laughed with a certain fruitiness. 'I often call it the Seven Pillars of Unwisdom.'

'Well, I wonder if you don't have something rather lighter?'

'All right. I tell you what. Try the elderflower. Delicious on a summer morning like this. Not unlike a Moselle.'

'Very well. I bow to your judgment.'

Miss Shuttleworth, having decided on a spot of five year old elderberry for herself, now found two tall wine glasses, filling one with the red wine and the other with the pale greenish elderflower. Lifting her glass towards the Professor she then said:

'Well, down the hatch. And many thanks, once again, for all your gifts.'

'Not at all. You see I have so much to spare, with that

large garden of mine and all those glass-houses – oh no,
I'm sorry, I didn't mean that. I didn't mean that at all.
What I meant was—'

The Professor broke off, shifted uneasily in his chair
and then took two hasty mouthfuls of wine as if either to
soothe or fortify his nerves.

'But the garden *is* large, isn't it?' Miss Shuttleworth
said. 'When I first came to live here, just before the war,
they employed twenty-two gardeners there. Then of
course, after the war, they pulled the mansion down and
now—'

At this point a certain gloom seemed to have settled
on the Professor. He sat in silence, lifting his lower lip and
gazing into his glass of elderflower wine. His thoughts
at that moment were with his garden. Truly it was large.
A great walled red-brick quadrangle housed six glass-
houses, partly in decay and sheltering grape-vines,
nectarines and peaches. Half cultivated, weedy beds of
earth nurtured impossibly large strips of asparagus,
rhubarb, sea-kale, artichokes, raspberries, strawberries
and black, red and white currants. It was totally impossible to know what to do with them all.

'You see,' the Professor said, 'nobody wanted a house
of that size. So down it came. And that's why I bought it
cheap.'

'And not because you wanted it?'

'Well, I wanted it in a way. I wanted to taste the country. After giving lectures for Heavens knows how long I
wanted to—'

'You live in the old keeper's cottage, don't you?'

The Professor merely nodded. An inability to frame a

coherent sentence of any kind merely served to increase his gloom. He gazed again at the elderflower wine, took a slow sip of it and then stared at the floor.

'You haven't said what you think of my elderflower,' Miss Shuttleworth said.

'Oh! delicious, delicious.'

'Drink up. Have a spot more.'

'No really, really. No thank you all the same.'

'Well, if you're not, I am. I've been up since five. I feel the need for a little alchoholic fortification.'

As Miss Shuttleworth got up to refill her glass with a generous portion of elderberry the Professor drew a deep breath, took a brief sip of his own wine and then said:

'So you wake early too, do you?'

'Invariably. Invariably.'

'I find those early hours so long drawn out, don't you?'

'Oh! never, never. On the contrary. They fly like the wind.'

'I wish I could say the same.'

Miss Shuttleworth now took a deep swig of her wine, gave her lips a slight smack of appreciation and then said:

'Tell me something. I've often wanted to ask this.'

'Yes?'

'What is philosophy? I mean what is it all about?'

For fully half a minute the Professor contemplated the floor, his grey eyes troubled. At last he said:

'Well, the word itself means – it's from the Greek – "fond of wisdom".'

Miss Shuttleworth laughed and drank her wine.

'Not my old Seven Pillars—'

'Well, no. Plato said that "philosophers are those who are able to grasp the eternal and the immutable. They are those who set their affections on that which in each case really exists.'

'Really? Sounds rather like me and my birds.'

'You're very fortunate. Objects of affection aren't always so easily come by.'

'No?'

'I'm afraid – but am I boring you?'

The Professor now, for the first time, looked straight at Miss Shuttleworth, seemed as if about to make some remark of importance and then remained dead silent.

'Why should you bore me?' Miss Shuttleworth said.

The Professor had no answer. He simply drained his glass and got to his feet.

'Oh! don't say you're going.'

'I fear so. I'd like to stay but—' a great sudden unpremediated rush of coherence overcame the Professor. 'Would you misunderstand me if I said that I'd like to stay for—'

The rush of coherence dried up as suddenly as it had begun. In the same moment the Professor seized his walking stick and rushed from the room.

Alone and in silence Miss Shuttleworth refilled her glass and sat for a time in thought. Then she got up, went over to the mantelpiece and looked in the mirror there. As people living alone often do she sometimes got into the habit of talking to herself.

'Well,' she said, raising her glass to her reflection in the mirror. 'Cheers.'

'Cheers about what?'

'Well, I suppose you might say you've just had a proposal.'

'Oh? Bit late in the day.'

'Better late than never I suppose.'

There, for a few moments, the conversation between her two sides ended. She sat looking dreamily, but also with a certain sadness, into the mirror. As she did so she found herself thinking of the Professor, the big impossible garden, the morning gifts on the doorstep and what the Professor had called 'those who set their affections on that which in each case really exists.'

At last she roused herself from these thoughts, took another deep swig of elderberry wine and then told herself that if she was going to make raspberry wine she'd better make a start. There was no fruit like raspberries for going mouldy quickly.

'Well, here goes—'

She took a final swig of wine, draining her glass.

'Or shall I make that damned jam?'

The Yellow Meads of Asphodel

'Indeed? May one ask who?'

'You may ask, of course. Roger Trenchard.'

He stared again, his cold blue eyes puzzled, and then asked who, if she didn't mind, was Roger Trenchard?

'Oh! don't say you've forgotten the Portmans' wedding. Roger was best man.'

'But good God, the Portmans' wedding was ten years ago.'

'Of course it was. And Julius Caesar made his first landing in England in 55 B.C. But that hasn't been forgotten.'

During all this exchange they hadn't once called each other darling; and now he said:

'And what caused Mr Trenchard suddenly to appear after all this time?'

She slowly sipped at champagne.

'He's just been made secretary of the County Nature Preservation Society.'

'And what, pray, has the preservation of Nature to do with you?'

'He's carrying out a survey of the Common.'

'Common? What Common? Not denominator?'

'Fairfield Common.'

And what, he asked, was so special about Fairfield Common?

'Oh! a great many things. It's fascinating. It has associations going back to the Bronze Age. It has all sorts of flora and things which you hardly find anywhere else in the county. Oh! it's fascinating.'

'Indeed?'

'Yes. He's going to take me round it next week and explain it all.'

He stared hard again.

'I think I'll go in and wash.'

'Won't you have a glass of champagne before you go? You can have my glass. I don't mind drinking out of Roger's.'

'I don't doubt it,' he said and strode away to the house to wash his hands.

'Yes, that's cotton grass.'

'Oh! how beautiful. It looks like little flakes of snow left over from winter.'

'Or feathers from a white bird.'

The delicate tufts of cotton grass, trembling in the light wind of a hot June morning, were very white against the wet dark peat bog.

'By August the bog will be covered with asphodel. All yellow.'

'That sounds lovely too. Isn't there a poem about it? "Fields of Asphodel" or something like that?'

'No, "meads of asphodel". Pope.' He quoted:

> ' "By those happy souls who dwell
> In yellow meads of asphodel".'

'How lovely.'

Roger Trenchard was a man of forty-five, thin and tall, with grave, gentle brown eyes and long-fingered hands that moved so quickly as to seem perpetually nervous. Virginia Claridge was so fascinated by these hands that now and then she lapsed into one of her listening trances, half as if expecting the hands, and not his voice, to do the talking.

'You see the bog never dries up. Even in the hottest summer. That's why we built this footbridge across it. No, it's perpetually wet – that's what makes it unique.'

At the far end of the wooden footbridge Roger Trenchard suddenly stopped, knelt down and then drew her attention to what might have been a group of little golden sea-anemones that could have mysteriously strayed in from the coast.

'How strange. What are they? Flowers?'

'Those are sun-dews. Can you see them moving?'

'They seem to have tiny little hands.'

'They're insectivorous. They catch flies.'

'No? Will we see them do it?'

'We might. On the other hand we might wait all day. It's like a lot of other things. You start watching and then nothing ever happens.'

'I'm prepared to wait all day.'

He stood upright, laughing quietly.

'Well, I must confess I'm not. Do you know it's one o'clock already? I could use a drink. Shall we walk as far as the *Blacksmiths Arms?* It's just down the road.'

'One o'clock? My goodness, we've been here three hours. It's gone like wildfire.'

In the bar of the *Blacksmiths Arms* she sat and sipped at whisky, several times confessing, yet again, that she couldn't believe how fast the morning had flown.

Roger Trenchard said he would confess to something too. He was raving hungry.

'They do quite good lunches here. I often drop in for mine. I wonder – would you join me today?'

'I'd love to.'

As they sat over lunch, sharing a bottle of Hock, she suddenly remembered something.

'Do forgive me. I forgot to ask how your wife is.'

'I lost her two years ago.'

'I'm so sorry.'

Over strawberries and cream she lapsed again into one of her listening trances.

'Brandy?' he said.

No, she thanked him all the same, but the wine was really enough.

'Oh! come on. Be a devil.' He laughed again. 'I'm going to. Keep me company.'

She laughed too.

'Oh! well, if you put it like that.'

He had parked his car back on the Common, under the shade of a huge Spanish chestnut tree. When she got into it she let her head rest, with a drowsy sigh, on the back of the seat; and then said that since it seemed to be a day for confessions she'd confess to something else.

'Today's been just about the nicest thing that's happaned to me for a long, long time.'

'I'll second that. It's been pretty nice for me too.'

Suddenly he quietly pressed his lips against the side of her forehead, letting them remain there for several moments.

'Was it the brandy kissing me just now? or simply you?'

'Simply me. And I hope not for the last time.'

With his quick nervous hands he suddenly held her face, kissing her full on the lips.

'Well, I'll make one more confession,' she said at last. 'I hope so too.'

It was past five o'clock when she got back to the big Edwardian house, happy and slightly drowsy still.

'Where on *earth* have you been?'

'You know quite well,' she said, 'where I've been. I've been exploring Fairfield Common with Roger Trenchard.'

'It seems to have taken an awful long time.'

'Naturally. There are over two hundred acres of it. There's a great deal to see.'

'I'm sure.'

Suddenly she seemed to lapse into a trance, but this time not of listening but reflection.

'Cotton grass and sun-dews and meads of asphodel.'

'What on *earth* are you talking about?'

'Have you ever seen a sun-dew? It's like a little golden sea-anemone. It's a flower that catches flies.'

'Does it indeed?'

'And the cotton grass looks like flakes of snow left over from winter, or feathers from a white bird.'

'Excuse me, I've some letters to write. And you might have said you were not coming back for lunch. Grace had cooked a chicken.'

'I'm sure you enjoyed it.'

'You might have telephoned.'

Head chilly and erect, he strode abruptly from the room.

After that she went up to her bedroom, slipped off her dress and lay down on the bed. In a few minutes she was deep in the sort of sleep that always evaded her night after night: wrapped in deep, heavy breathing, utterly tranquil.

When she finally woke it was nearly eight o'clock. For some minutes she lay staring at the ceiling, wondering where she was, what time of day it was and whether the day behind her was reality or dream. Then finally she remembered it all again, but now sharply, brilliantly magnified: the cotton grass, the sun-dew, the wine, the brandy and the meads of asphodel. She also remembered something else: it was all going to be repeated, a second time, the following day.

She and her brother always had dinner very formally, every evening, in the big dining-room. Grace, the housekeeper cook, a plump woman of middle age who rarely spoke unless spoken to, always laid out on the large round mahogany table the silver cutlery, the silver salt-cellars, the silver pepper and mustard pots, the silver wine-coasters and the silver candlesticks, together with the wine glasses and the central vase of flowers, in the same traditional fashion that had gone on for years. In addition to all the other silver there was also a little silver bell and this Virginia Claridge rang in order to summon Grace between the courses.

That evening she duly rang it, as usual, after the soup. For a good ten minutes, most unusually, there was no answer.

'Where the devil *is* that woman? She's been getting terribly slack lately. She's never damn well here when you want her.'

'I hadn't noticed it.'

'Then all I can say is you're singularly unobservant.'

'Perhaps I am. But there's no need to be irritable about it.'

'I am not irritable!'

'All I can say is it sounds remarkably like it. Don't fret – she'll come.'

'She damn well better. And quick.'

A minute later Grace arrived in the dining-room carrying the fish course, shyly and confusedly apologetic.

'Grace, where on *earth* have you been? We must have been waiting at least a quarter of an hour.'

'I'm sorry, sir. I'm terribly sorry. But just as I was getting the fish ready a messenger boy arrived with some flowers.'

'Flowers? Flowers? Who on *earth* for?'

'Miss Virginia, sir.'

'Good God. Did you order flowers, Virginia?'

'No.'

'There was this note pinned to them,' Grace said. 'They're carnations. All colours. About four dozen of them I should say.'

Virginia Claridge took the note that Grace handed to her. Her brother was silent and stiff as she opened it.

Then as she read the note she suddenly flushed, deeply, from the throat upwards.

'Well, who's the extravagant donor?'

'They're from Roger Trenchard.'

'Fast worker I must say.'

She leapt sharply to her feet.

'That,' she said, 'is a fatuous, puerile and contemptible remark.'

She started to stride, trembling, from the room.

'Where are you going? Aren't you going to finish your dinner?'

'I do not,' she said, 'feel like eating. I prefer the harmless company of my room.'

In the kitchen she hastily arranged the huge bouquet of carnations in a vase and then took them to her bedroom. There she poured herself a recklessly large whisky, but her hands were trembling so much from both excitement and anger that she spilt a good quarter of it down her dress. Hastily she then drank the rest of it and then filled the glass to the top again.

For the next half hour or so she sat impotently in a trance, not now either of listening or reflection but of both joy and fury. The sight of the carnations in their many variations of red and yellow and white and orange several times moved her so much that, near to tears, she buried her face in her hands. Several times too she renewed her whisky.

After about an hour of this, not quite fully conscious of what she was doing, she leapt up and went unsteadily downstairs. There, in the dining-room, after his customary fashion, her brother was calmly sipping a glass of port. Instantly inflamed by this, she actually raised her voice.

'If you do not apologise for that remark I shall in future take all my meals in my own room. I will not sit here and be spoken to like a dog.'

Her brother, silent, merely sipped at his port.

'*Are you, or are you not, going to apologise?*' She was now actually shouting.

'I see nothing to apologise for.'

'*Are you going to apologise?*' she yelled.

'Good God, you sound as if you might be drunk.'

'Which, in all probability, is what I am. Moreover I profoundly hope the condition will be permanent. It may help to relieve the strain of undergoing penal servitude with you.'

At this she turned and started unsteadily for the door. Then at the door she suddenly remembered something and turned back to say:

'Oh! and one more thing. I had in fact invited Roger Trenchard to dinner tomorrow night. I shall now cancel it. I wouldn't want him to have the unpleasant experience of eating with a pig.'

Her brother merely toyed with his glass of port. This further infuriated her so much that she shouted:

'And don't forget this, you smug insulter. Hell hath no fury like a woman scorned!'

After that she went upstairs, drank more whisky and then lay on her bed for a long, long time, weeping bitter, scalding tears.

* * *

Not once, after that, did she appear at dinner. When she didn't take it in her room she took it, at some country pub, a restaurant or at his own cottage, with Roger Trenchard. Sometimes, when the evenings were fine and warm, they didn't even bother with the formality of a meal. She would make sandwiches, he would bring a bottle of wine and then they would wander across the Common, across stretches of heather and asphodel now in pink and yellow flower, until they found some dry, secluded place to picnic. When the food and wine were both finished they lay down together in long and often completely silent embrace, exchanging long, all-consuming kisses or simply staring up at the sky until the first specks of stars began to break the twilight.

On one particularly humid August night he said:

'Did you know that the whole character of this common has completely changed? There was a big fire here about twenty years ago. It changed the entire life of the place.'

'Ah! yes, I remember that fire. It burned for weeks.'

'Months. It was really the peat burning. Underground. It was a long, hot summer, rather like this one, and when the fire was out nothing was the same any more.'

'Rather like you and my life.'

'The refiners' fire?'

'That's a nice way of putting it. Yes, the refiners' fire.'

'I wonder which it's nicest to be? The refiner or the refined?'

'The refined isn't complaining.'

'Nor, I may say, is the refiner.'

'Oh! God, you're so marvellous to me.'

That night they lay there until long after darkness was complete. By midnight the air had scarcely cooled and it was about that time that he said:

'You said I was marvellous to you. I could be even more marvellous.'

'I utterly fail to see how.'

'I could make love to you.'

She lay quiet, in one of her many forms of entrancement, scarcely daring to breathe.

'Have you ever made love?'

'How could I? There's never ever been anyone to make love to me.'

'I see.'

'I've had to exist with brotherly love. And now even that's gone the way of all flesh.'

'Love *is* the way of all flesh.'

'That's a nice way of putting it.'

He laughed and said:

'It must be getting late. How about coming back to the cottage for a night-cap?'

'That's also a nice way of putting it,' she said and laughed too.

For a time, at the cottage, they sat more or less in silence, drinking whisky. Then at last he put down his glass, gently unzipped her dress and one by one drew her breasts free. The firm beauty of them not only surprised him but threw him into such an entrancement of his own that he was moved to kiss them.

In a further entrancement of her own she simply had nothing to say and it was finally he who spoke:

'Do you have to go home tonight?'

'Logically I suppose I do.'

'Love isn't logical.'

'No.' He was caressing her breasts now and she was trembling. 'You were right the first time. It is the way of all flesh.'

Upstairs she entreated him to be tender with her.

'Because,' she said, 'I feel like – oh! I don't know – I suppose – Oh! I suppose it sounds silly. But I feel like—'

'Like what?'

'One of "those happy souls who dwell in yellow meads of asphodel".'

When she got back home the following morning, about half-past ten, still slightly dazed with happiness, she found her brother standing on the front doorstep of the house. His hands were rigidly clasped behind his back, as if they might have been holding an invisible weapon with which to chastise a recalcitrant truant or a deserter. His bony face was not merely grim. It was part of a piece of statuary, hardened by pain.

'Am I to suppose you've been out all night?'

His voice too was hard: the voice, almost, of a man opening a court-martial.

'On the contrary. I've been *in* all night.'

'In? Where?'

'Bed.'

She moved to go into the house. He barred the way.

'I think I've a right to know where,' he said.

'Really? Are you your sister's keeper?'

'We've always been very close. Now you've deserted me.'

'Not yet,' she said. 'But I propose to. May I now go into the house? I'd like some coffee.'

He stood firm, impotent, hard, face still a piece of statuary grim with pain.

'I presume all this has something to do with Mr Trenchard?'

'You presume quite correctly.'

'You seem to have lost your head. I should have thought at your age you'd have known better.'

'Emotions have nothing to do with age. I happen to be in love with him.'

'Love? What do you know about love? You've never been in love in your life.'

'Nor have I ever eaten caviare. But that's no reason why I shouldn't try it. And perhaps find it delicious.'

Speechless now, he merely made a sound between a grunt and a snarl.

'And another thing. Since we are exchanging pleasantries you might as well know that I am going to be married. And very soon. Then the desertion will be complete. Now will you have the decency to let me go into the house?'

Still unable to speak, he stood biting his lip, his face agonised.

'I really would like some coffee. Do you mind?'

'Virginia, don't let's quarrel. We've never quarrelled. I can't bear it.'

'You might ask yourself who began the quarrel. And perhaps, if you come up with an answer, you'll let me know.'

'But you hardly know this man. How can you be sure you'll be happy?'

'I've never been so happy in my life. I'm one of "those happy souls who dwell in yellow meads of asphodel".'

'I simply don't understand you lately. It isn't the first time you've talked to me in riddles.'

'Perhaps it's because you fail to understand that there may be more than one woman inside a body.'

He could find no possible answer to this and stood aside, at last, to let her into the house. There she asked Grace to make her coffee and then, when it was ready, took it up to her room. Sitting there, by the window, drinking it, she stared out over the August garden brilliant with dahlias, phlox, verbena, golden rod and still many roses, without really seeing them. What she was really seeing were stars of sun-dew and the trembling flowers of asphodel.

Nor did she give any thought to the quarrel with her brother; it was a thing of pettiness that she had already thrown aside like a piece of soiled and unwanted paper. She was thinking instead of the way her breasts had been caressed, then kissed, then caressed again; she was thinking of her first experience of love and of how, when she woke in the morning, it had been repeated, longer and more beautifully.

* * *

All this time she was unaware that, downstairs, at first in his study, then during several walks in the garden, her brother brooded. His particular broodiness was not of anger; it didn't even arise from any bitterness of the words they had exchanged. It was a bitterness of gnawing jealousy, of the pain of a man who had lost a lover, even a wife, to a rival contender. Several times this so affected him that he was near to tears and by the end of the morning near to despair.

By that time he had taken refuge in his sister's remedy. When Grace finally announced that lunch was ready he replied that he wanted none. He was in fact in his study, silently lunching off whisky.

There Virginia found him.

'Aren't you coming for lunch?'

'I am not.'

'Then I'll ask Grace to clear it away. I'm going out to lunch with Roger. He's just come to fetch me in his car.'

'What time will you be back?'

'I haven't the remotest, faintest idea. As I said before, are you your sister's keeper?'

'I used to think I was.'

He drank deeply at his whisky. Then he turned to entreat her not to quarrel with him, to say at last that he was sorry and how he could no longer bear it all; but by the time he had set down his glass and was ready to speak his sister was no longer there.

He brooded for another hour and several more whiskies. Then somewhere about mid-afternoon he got up, left his study and paused at the kitchen to tell Grace that he was going out, up through the wood, to shoot pigeons. There were more of them than ever; they were a confounded nuisance on the corn.

He walked through the wood with his gun. At the end of the path was a stile and beyond the stile a field of wheat, still uncut and burnt brown in ear.

He stood staring at the wheatfield for some minutes with pained eyes, as if not really seeing it, and then rested the stock of the gun on the step of the stile, at the same time tucking the two barrels under his throat.

At the violent sound of the double shot a great cloud of rooks rose from the field of wheat, black and frightened, and flew wailing far into the sky.

A Taste of Blood

D ILLON woke with all his senses bruised and drugged, breathing heavily, unable to remember where he was.

The tortured impression that he had been lying unconscious on the bed for some long time, perhaps a day, changed harshly to raging pain. He was suddenly frightened by a ghastly conviction that his left arm had been severed just below the elbow and that the raw flesh was still hanging by a thread.

He sat up slowly. His head turned and throbbed like a ponderous roundabout. At times it seemed actually to click. Then it stopped momentarily and turned again, sickly. He shut his eyes, opened them glassily and slowly made several odd discoveries, the first of which was that he was still in his shirt and trousers. The second was that he had still one shoe on, the third that from top to bottom his left shirt sleeve was stiff as brown paper with thick dried blood.

He swung his feet slowly to the floor and sat for some minutes with his head buried in his hands. It wasn't as if he had been drunk the night before; he was somehow sure of that. It was more as if he had dragged up and down great slopes, among battering rocks. Every limb had a

savage sprain in it; his head seemed to have been merci-
lessly banged by boulders.

Even when he at last stood up and looked at himself in
the mirror hanging over the wash-stand he still found it
utterly impossible to remember a fraction of anything
that had happened to him. He hadn't the remotest idea
of what day it was. He was unaware of the time of day;
or how long he had been lying there with the arm oozing
blood. His right cheek-bone had a sulphurous green
bruise curled poisonously round it, oddly enough in the
shape of a rough question mark. His thick black hair was
matted with blood too. His left ear looked like a lump of
red offal half-chewed by a dog.

In bitter pain he stripped off his shirt and made the
further discovery that his arm was slit to the bone outside
the crook of the elbow. It took him ten minutes or so to
wash the arm free of blood and another ten minutes to
wash the blood out of his hair and clean up the lacerated
left ear. Sometimes he spat into the wash-basin. Clots of
blood streaked from his mouth and the taste of blood was
bitter too.

His ear, when washed, wasn't exactly painful. It
merely burned like a dynamo. It caused him also to be
deaf on his left side. As a result, when he walked about
the room looking for a clean shirt and a jacket, he walked
lop-sided, half off balance, like a drunk.

Dressed at last, he stood staring out of the window.
His van, a small dark green one, stood slewed diagonally
across the yard, the driving door still open. He couldn't
remember anything about that either.

He went slowly downstairs. The back door was

unlocked. Sunlight streamed across the yard. The metal of the van door was hot to the touch. He got the impression that the time was late afternoon.

Suddenly he was afflicted by a great thirst. He longed for a beer, a beer that would be endlessly deep and cold. He crawled into the van seat and then, after starting up the engine, discovered that he could scarcely crook his left arm.

He was forced to drive one-handed down the half-mile hill to the village. He was twenty-eight, a slow, mild, rather awkward giant of a man, easy going, obliging, unquarrelsome, eager to please. He would do any kind of job for anybody at any time. In winter he cut chestnut poles. In spring he did hop-stringing. In summer there was cherry-picking and in September a month in the hop-gardens.

Hop-gardens? For a fraction of a second he remembered something about hop-gardens, then his mind was blank again. He stopped the van and sat staring down the street, trying to think. He was outside the *Black Horse* and the door was open. Then he knew it was after six o'clock.

He got out of the van and went up the stone steps of the *Black Horse* and into the bar. He hung on to the edge of the counter, half-faint with the exertion of climbing the steps. Joe Stevens was alone behind the bar, wiping glasses. The image of Joe swam about a bit but at least he knew it was Joe. That was something. He remembered Joe.

'Give me a beer, Joe, will you?'

Joe, shocked, staring hard, pulled the beer. A mass of froth overflowed yeastily across the brown counter.

Dillon took the glass and held it to his lips. Suddenly he didn't want the beer. His thirst was violent as ever but underneath and behind it all his body felt white and frail with sickness. He set the glass back on the bar and said:

'Joe, where was I last night?'

'You wasn't in here.'

'No? Where was I?'

'You wasn't in here all night. What's happened to you? God Almighty, Dillon, what hit you?'

'I dunno. I can't remember. Where the hell was I?'

Joe stood mopping up the last of the froth from the bar.

'Last time I saw you was when you drove past here last night. Six o'clock that was. Dead on. I know because I was just opening up, just unbolting the door.'

'Six o'clock?'

'Yes. You had a girl in the front seat with you.'

'Girl?'

'Yes. I thought it was funny. I said to Edna "that's funny. Dillon with a girl. You don't often see Dillon with girls".'

'Girl? What girl?'

'Biggish girl. Fair. Wearing orange-coloured slacks. I didn't get a good look at her last night but I did this morning.'

'This morning?'

'She was in here this morning. About twelve o'clock. Asking for you. They told her up in the gardens she might find you here.'

'Up in the gardens? Is that where she was?'

'Started Monday she told me.'

'Monday? What's today?'

'Wednesday.'

Dillon took a slow drink of beer. His sickness receded a little. His body seemed less frail and white. He dwelt for half a minute on a blurred image of the hop-gardens, the figure of a girl slowly taking vague shape in it, cloudy and except for one detail unfamiliar.

'Wear a sort of band round her head? Blue, I think.'

'That's her,' Joe said. 'That's her.'

Dillon drove out of the village, back up the hill. The hop-gardens, a quarter stripped of vine, lay in three oblongs across the south slope of a valley. On the far side of the valley hills white with late barley lay crested by great summer-scorched woods, the upper edges of the trees already burnt to ginger, giving them the look of old, moulting bear skins.

He was still wondering whether to drive the van into the gardens or leave it on the road and walk the last hundred yards or so when he saw the girl walking down the hill. She was weaving the same orange slacks and the same bright blue band round her hair. Her shirt was the same colour as the band and her feet were in yellowish-brown sandals.

As soon as she saw him stop the van she started running. She was big in every detail, without being massive or heavy. The strong smooth thighs reminded him of a mare's and her brown-blonde hair, thick and held down by the band, was like a mane.

'God, there you are. Where have you been all day? I've been looking for you everywhere.'

She snatched open the van door, got into the seat beside and took one wide shocked look at him.

'God, your face. Your face! Whatever happened to your face?'

'Dunno. Can't remember. Must have had a crash with the van.'

She gave a brief bitter laugh that shocked his mild and unaggressive nature almost as much as the first sight of his battered face had done.

'Van, my foot. They did it. It's just like Iris said. Somebody gave them the tip. Somebody phoned them.'

He groped through clouds of dark bewilderment. He said he didn't think he knew quite what she was on about. Iris? Who was Iris? Who were they?

'Iris is my girl-friend. We work in Stepney together. We came down here to get a breath of fresh air.'

'Who are they then?'

She looked quickly up and down the road.

'I don't think we'd better stop here talking. We'd better go somewhere else. Where you took me last night. Let's go there.'

'Where was that?'

'Don't you remember? Up on the hills there. You don't remember? There was a big wood and we pulled inside. There was a hedge with honeysuckle on it. I didn't know what it was and you picked a bit for me. You don't remember?'

He said he didn't remember. Not only that part but

all the other parts. Not a thing. It was all a blank. He'd
had a job even to remember her.

'Let's go,' she said. 'It'll be quieter there.' A big
scarlet petrol tanker drove past, setting up a great wash
of air that started all the skeins of hops swaying across the
gardens like pale green curtains. 'No. I don't think we'd
better. Can you think of somewhere else? Somewhere
quiet and out of sight? Off the road?'

He sat staring at the dashboard, his left hand on the
ignition key, trying hard to do his first real coherent
piece of thinking of the day. After almost half a minute a
gap opened in the deep clouds of his confusion and he
said:

'Up in the old sand quarry. That ought to do. Nobody
ever goes up there.'

'That sounds all right. Let's go up there.'

He paused for a few seconds longer before attempting
to turn the ignition key.

'We could go back to my place. You must be hungry.
We could get you something to eat.'

'I'm not hungry,' she said. 'I'd rather be out in the
fresh air anyway. I feel freer outside. Besides, they know
where you live by now. It wouldn't be any good going
there.'

She gave him a look of sudden tenderness, urging him
to get started, at the same time giving his left arm a
sudden squeeze of affection. In agony he let out a gasp of
pain and at last, sick to the core of himself, turned the
key.

'Now see if you can't remember. What did you do
when you left me last night? Outside the hop-gardens.'

He sat in the car, staring across the old deserted sand quarry. It formed a sort of arena, a hundred and fifty yards across, its walls rising thirty or forty feet in a rough circle like cliffs of rough, amber-coloured cheese. A shaggy fringe of burnt grass grew from the top and here and there big stumpy elderberry trees had taken root in gaps among the stone. The floor of it was like some arid bone-yard, completely flat and white, from which a flood had swept the bones away. From scores of holes in the cliffs dark clouds of sand-martins poured and swooped, crying thinly.

'You kissed me good-night and then went down the hill. It must have been half past ten. Perhaps eleven.'

'Kissed you good-night?'

She gave a short laugh and quickly brushed her lips across his own.

'Yes. Kissed. Like that, only better. You don't even remember that, do you?'

He had once again to confess that he didn't remember.

'Do you remember anything about being followed by a motor-bike? Perhaps two motor-bikes? Perhaps three? Does that mean anything to you?'

No: that didn't mean anything to him either.

'Tell me,' he said, 'who they are.'

'I'm not sure how many there were yet.' she said. 'Three at least. Perhaps five. So I wouldn't know who they were. But I know one for sure.'

'Yes?'

'He's a fellow named Tooley.' She made a movement as if to hold his arm and then remembered the pain of the previous time. 'I may as well tell you. I was friends with him. Then he started to get big. Big-headed. Big-mouthed. Swelled-headed. The lot. Then he swizzed my brother out of seventy quid on a motor-bike deal. Then went about boasting of it, shooting his fat mouth. He's as mad as a monkey about motor-bikes. They all are.'

The talk of motor-bikes entered Dillon's mind with the sudden click of a key. It seemed, he thought, that he might be on the verge of remembering things.

'So we had one big hell of a stack-up. I told him I'd never see him again and I damn well meant it too. He started to rough me up then – that's all he knows about, roughing people up – but I hammered him back again. He knows I'm not scared of him. You don't have to be if you get on that flaming bike with him. I know.'

Dillon sat thinking again of motor-bikes. A raw note of fast engines searing up a hill scorched the vague distances of his memory. Across the quarry a huge segment of shadow lay almost black against the brilliant face of sand.

'Got a cigarette?' she said suddenly. 'I don't smoke much since this cancer scare. But I could do with one now.'

He fumbled in his pockets. He brought out half a packet of cigarettes and a lighter. He sprang the lighter catch and it flamed the first time.

'Thanks,' she said and blew smoke.

'You'd better hold on to the lighter,' Dillon said. 'You might want it again.'

'Just thought of something,' she said. She slipped the lighter from one hand to the other and back again. 'Bet you don't remember my name.'

'I thought it was Shirley.'

She laughed. It was a friendly, deep sound.

'First thing you asked me. Said you liked it. Thought it suited me. Olga, not Shirley.'

'You must think I'm a damn fool.'

'You looked at me all afternoon,' she said. 'I could feel you out of the back of my head. I can see you now. You were riding on the back of that trailer and every time you went by I had a funny sort of feeling you wanted me. You remember all that, surely, or don't you?'

All of a sudden he saw her again as he had seen her all the golden afternoon in the hop-garden, his memory absolutely bright. He could see her big sun-reddened arms pulling at the bine. She was looking at him with large bee-brown eyes and the orange slacks were stretched tight across her thighs.

'I remember now,' Dillon said. 'It's all starting to come back.'

'Remember anything else?' she said. 'About last night, I mean?'

In an almost explosive flash that too came back. The searing roar of motor-bike engines dinned itself cruelly into his consciousness. He was driving home in darkness down the hill. A bike suddenly came up at great speed beside him, cutting so fast across his head-lights that he braked and swerved. Then it stuck in front of him, full in his head-lights, never more than five or six yards away. Then a second bike came roaring up beside him and he could hear a third at his back.

He saw the faces of the first two riders grinning with

wide leers under their black crash helmets. He remembered yelling madly, shaking his fist out of the window. Every now and then he accelerated and then they accelerated too. They had him trapped in a sort of mobile vice. There was no escaping. And finally when he stopped they too stopped. They had him caught as if he were a criminal on the run and the first thing he saw on getting out of the driving seat was the swing of a big spanner in the lights of the van.

Slowly he told her all this. She listened without a word. He was still distraught and bewildered by the naked recollection of the first spanner blow crashing against his ear and all he could ask was:

'Who'd want to do a thing like that to me? What have I done? I was just going home. Minding my own business.'

She threw her cigarette out of the window. She played tensely with the lighter, tipping it from hand to hand.

'Somebody must have told them. Like I said, somebody must have phoned.' She suddenly let out a half-shout. Her voice was savage. 'Iris. Nobody could have done it only Iris. My friend, the jealous bitch, my friend. God, what a blasted fool I've been. What a blasted, cock-eyed fool.'

She rammed a second cigarette into her mouth. She struck the lighter into flame and then lit the cigarette, her fingers shaking with anger.

'We'd better go,' she said. 'I got to have a few words with Iris. I got things to say to that bitch. My friend.'

*   *   *

Dillon supposed they must have travelled less than half a mile from the sand quarry when her ears, far sharper than his, suddenly picked up the sound of bike engines from some distance behind. A second after she heard it she shouted:

'Turn off! It mightn't be them but turn off all the same. Is there some other way back to the quarry? We'd be out of sight there.'

'Think so. I'll take the next turn.'

Dillon drove faster, half skidding round the next turn. In another two minutes a thick chestnut copse cut off all sight of the road behind. From under the dark chestnut leaves the wind blew cool into the windows of the car, but he could feel sweat pouring down his face, stinging the smashed raw flesh of his ear.

Suddenly she picked up the sound of bikes again, roaring past the turn.

'Five of them this time. Two big Nortons in front. I'd know them anywhere.'

Dillon stepped hard on the accelerator pedal. In the confusion he was having some difficulty in remembering the road. Beyond the chestnut copses was a field of late wheat, half-cut, a big red combine harvester standing in its centre, and beyond that a farm.

Suddenly he remembered a back-cut, not much more than a cart-track, behind the farm. He slowed down and swerved into it and in another five minutes he could see once again the rough, amber-coloured cliffs of sand.

He stopped the car and switched off the engine. His face was running with a heavy sweat of weakness. He had an overwhelming desire to get out of the car and walk about and drink fresh air but he suddenly knew his legs would never carry him.

She suddenly recognised the fresh agony of his weakness and drew down his head and let it rest on her shoulder. She got a handkerchief and wiped some of his sweat away. Once her thick hair fell across his face and the act of its falling drew a curtain across his memory, so that for a second time he didn't know where he was.

He was shaken out of this half-coma by her sitting up with a violent jerk. She could hear the bikes again, she said, and this time her voice was a whisper.

'Where?'

'I can hear them coming up the hill. They're going back now they couldn't find you.'

He saw her with vague eyes. She was tense, her face taut with the strain of listening. Soon the sound of engines was so loud that he could even hear it himself. The bikes, it seemed to him, roared across the mouth of the quarry. The walled arena was battered with echoes.

Then it was suddenly quiet: oddly and unhealthily quiet, like the quiet after sudden thunder.

'They've gone,' he said, his mind still too vague to notice that she didn't answer.

Through sheer weakness his head dropped again on her shoulder. This time she made no attempt to touch it. She sat upright, braced as if to receive a blow. Then suddenly she half leapt to the window, leaning out.

'Oh! my God. Like I thought,' she said.

'What is it? What's up?'

'They're here. Five of them. Over there.'

A single bike started to come at slow and sinister speed

across the sand. The remaining four lined up behind, engines ticking over, closing the gap in the quarry.

The bike came up to the van and stopped. The figure riding it was a big, crusty fellow with a square jaw. His crash helmet was black. His leather driving coat was black too. A skull and cross-bones was painted in white across the back of it. He seemed about nineteen.

'Well, if it ain't our Olga. Well, well. Long time no see.'

'Buzz off. Make yourself scarce.'

'I only just got here. How's the boy friend? Looks nice and healthy to me.'

'How'd you know we were here?'

'Funny, really. Little accident of nature. You know. We thought it looked like a good place to water the horses.'

'Buzz off. Go on, buzz. Get lost. Before I lose my temper.'

'Now, now. If you don't mind your manners, little lady, I might mark you.'

She played with the lighter. She clenched it in her right fist in such a way that the nozzle protruded through the two centre knuckles.

'And there might be ways of marking you too, big-head. Now buzz. Start motoring.'

'Billy Boy looks bone-lazy to me. Boy friend looks tired. I thought you like strong blokes? Country boy needs exercise. Start driving, country boy.'

'Driving?' Dillon said. 'Where?'

'Just round. Just round and round and round and round. Till me and the boys tell you to stop. Won't be long. Couple of hours or so. I've got time.'

Dillon, almost too weak to hold the wheel, hesitated.

'Better drive,' she said. 'This one's the big strong man. He loves odds. Five to one. He loves that. Tell me something. Did Iris phone you? Was it that jealous bitch?'

'Iris?' he said. 'Who's Iris? Never heard of her. Drive.'

Dillon started to drive. Only two bikes now guarded the entrance to the quarry. Like evil black beetles, the other three took up the escort of the van, one on each flank, the other three or four yards ahead. Now and then the three black helmeted riders signalled Dillon to go faster. On the cramped circle of the quarry floor they hotted the speed up to thirty, then forty and beyond. To Dillon it seemed like fifty. He drove as in a drunken daze, his head battered by engine roar, his vision bewildered by the wild flight of frightened martins crying everywhere.

After the fifth or sixth circuit they thought up a trick. Each time the van turned westward the slanting sun drove shafts of light flat into Dillon's eyes, dazzling him. Half-blind, he struggled desperately to keep the van upright. He drove as into a blazing arc-light, each rider in turn jinking in front of him, swerving, half-horizontal, like a dirt-track rider, dragging feet, raising searing white dust against his screen.

He now began to drive in a sheer suspense of terror. He lost all count of the number of circuits. Only half-conscious, he presently felt himself to be performing in a wall of death, in a dusty nightmare, on some hellish fairground. In his terrified concentration on the blinding dust in front of him he was no longer even aware of the girl.

It must have been at the twentieth circuit or so that his head seemed half to fall from his shoulders and the entire face of the quarry turned black. The girl shouted and grabbed the wheel. A second later a jinking rider sliced in front of her and she drove straight at him, the engine stalling violently as she cut him down.

In a flash she was out of the van, the cigarette lighter in her hand, already alight. Tooley lay half pinned under the big Norton, petrol pouring from the carburettor.

She stood two yards from him, holding the lighter at arm's length.

'Now will you buzz? or shall I put it to the carburettor?'

'Don't be a bloody fool! Take it away! I don't want to burn!'

'Then call them off from me!' The other two riders were beetling madly up from behind the van. 'Call them off, I tell you, or I'll throw it. I don't mind burning. I'll burn. I'm not scared of that. Call them off, I tell you!'

She raised the lighter high above her head as if to throw it. Tooley actually screamed, yelling for the bike to be lifted off from him.

'That's right,' she said. 'Lift his cradle. Take him away in his cradle now.'

The other two riders pulled the bike from Tooley, who swung fiercely back into the saddle, white and savage.

'I've a good mind to run you down for that, lady.'

She held the lighter out to him, like a torch.

'Yes?' she said. 'Try.'

Ten seconds later a slow procession of three bikes started across the sand. It joined the other two at the gap and went on like a dusty cortège to the road.

The girl went back to the van and sat with Dillon. The sun began to go down. Without a word she drew his head on to her shoulder and kissed his face. For a long time he had neither the strength nor the will to say a word either but finally he moved and brushed his mouth against her own.

'It'll soon be dark,' she said. 'Think you can drive?'

'Think so.'

'Take it steady,' she said. 'Take it easy. You think there might be time to gather me a piece of honeysuckle? It might do something to sweeten the air.'

Dillon leaned his head out of the window, breathing hard.

'It feels sweet to me already,' he said.

He started the engine. With pain he drove slowly forward and once again the air was filled with a crying tumult of wings.

The Love Letters of Miss Maitland

O<small>N</small> a prematurely dark, rainy evening in April, Miss Gladys Maitland sat down in her bedsitter, alone, to write – or rather type – the last of her many letters to herself. She had written the first, the only one which she had failed to keep with all the rest, a little under two years before.

She well remembered the circumstances that led up to that first letter. For some months previously she had begun to suffer from an illusion that she was ill – perhaps very ill, even incurably ill. A small indefinable pain in her left side gradually magnified itself to something that seemed to spell malignancy. In turn this led to sleeplessness, which in turn brought on periods of lassitude where she no longer cared whether she ate or not. These in turn led to nausea, which then brought on headaches of melancholic and sometimes paralysing pain.

It never once occurred to her that these things had anything at all to do with Mrs Braithwaite, her companion typist at the office. Mrs Braithwaite was a singularly good-looking girl, with sensationally smooth golden hair and light blue eyes immensely radiant with the ecstasies of recent marriage.

Before the marriage she and Miss Maitland had been

intimate friends, sharing a small flat together. With selfless joy Miss Maitland did all the washing, ironing, cooking, bed making and so on for the two of them: tasks of willing, silent, affectionate devotion. She asked for nothing in return. The friendship and beauty of Mrs Braithwaite alone was reward enough for her.

Now she had moved to the bedsitter. The many little devoted tasks that had given her such joy were no longer needed. Moreover Mrs Braithwaite, on whom marriage had bestowed an aura of radiance that positively seemed to shimmer like a heat haze on some summer horizon, seemed greatly to have changed. As from some nuptial ivory tower she seemed now to look down on Miss Maitland, pityingly, even with the slightest scorn.

Constantly Miss Maitland was made to feel more painfully aware of the drabness, the inadequacy, of the bedsitter. The brand-new curtains of Mrs Braithwaite's brand-new house were of yellow wild silk; the olive-green flock wallpaper was the most expensive in the book; the fridge, the television set, the car, the carved pine mantelpiece, the Chinese carpets – all were symbols of a world utterly remote from Miss Maitland, which she could never hope to share.

Nevertheless, eventually, Miss Maitland felt compelled to speak to Mrs Braithwaite of her fear of illness. Mrs Braithwaite listened with bored tolerance, then cool indifference and finally with open impatience.

'Perhaps if you didn't think about it quite so much—'
'I'm sure I don't think of it all that much.'
Well, it's the mental attitude that matters. In any case you're so worried, why don't you see your doctor?'

The greater fear of having fears confirmed ran sharply through Miss Maitland like another pain. She confessed she hated the thought of a surgery.

'It's probably all imagination,' Mrs Braithwaite said, and though her voice was slightly superior, cool and acid, she actually laughed too. 'You know, *la malade imaginaire.*'

Miss Maitland could hardly be called drab. She simply lacked lustre. She always wore her mole-coloured hair in a net. Her legs were straight and thick and her eyes had something of the appearance of small brown snails.

When she arrived at the doctor's surgery a surprise awaited her. 'I've always seen Dr Cameron . . . '

'I'm Dr O'Brien.' A thin young man, with brilliant brown eyes and hair that seemed to spark at every tip with a gingery point of fire, spoke with a scarcely detectable Irish brogue. 'Dr Cameron has retired.'

'Oh, really. I didn't know.'

'Well, first let me have your name.'

'Maitland.'

'Miss? And Christian name?'

'Gladys.'

'Age?'

'Thirty-five.'

At the doctor's request, after a few more questions, she slipped off her dress and lay down on a couch. Suddenly unaccountably nervous, she felt the first touch

C

of the stethoscope on her chest like a knife stab. She started to breathe heavily and went on to answer more questions as in a dream.

'Do you sleep well?'

No, she had to confess she didn't. On the whole she slept very badly.

'Do you take anything for it? Pills or anything?'

No, she didn't. She always had a glass of hot milk last thing, though it didn't seem to help very much.

'What about recreation? Do you swim? Tennis or anything like that?'

No, she didn't do anything. She read quite a lot. She liked walking too.

Then the questions became more intimate. 'What about boy friends?'

The question caused a startling convulsion deep in her chest. The stethoscope ceased its travelling over her rather inconspicuous breasts and at the doctor's request she turned over and lay face downwards. From that position the voice of the doctor seemed to come to her from a great distance, with a kind of mesmeric quietness.

'I'll give you some sleeping tablets. They're not habit-forming, but never take more than two at a time.'

She thanked him. But what of the pain?

'When did you last have a holiday?'

Last September, she said. She always took it in September.

'Is there any reason why you shouldn't take a couple of weeks off now, a month or two earlier?' She didn't suppose there was. She'd try.

'Yes, do that.' The doctor gave a short, light laugh.

For some reason the upward lilt in his voice struck her as being like the bright leap of a fish out of dark water. 'Have you never been to my country? To Ireland?'

Never, she said. As a matter of fact, she usually went to London. She liked the museums and the theatres.

The doctor laughed again, his voice now captivatingly rich as well as bright. 'I tell you what. There's this little place down in Kerry, not far from the Kenmare river. I'll write it down for you, and the little hotel there. It's kept by a Mrs Cassidy. If you tell her you know me, it'll be like the gates of heaven opening for you.'

She was moved by this to make a reply so near to being jocular that it surprised her into laughing, too. 'I don't think I want them opening quite so soon as all that, Doctor.'

'Ah yes, bad metaphor. But I tell you, you'll eat fresh brown trout there with lashings of butter that'll melt like manna in your mouth, and raspberries with cream so thick you could stand a flagpole upright in it. And the sunsets over the bay . . . ah, they're like apricots – pure gold apricots with just a touch of red on their cheeks.'

While saying all this, he was writing out the prescription for her sleeping tablets and she was putting on her dress. Now he got up from his desk and saw that she was struggling with the zip. Casually he helped her with it, his fingers brushing her bare back with a brief lightness that prompted all her inner trembling again.

'Well, there's the address of Mrs Cassidy's hotel and there's your prescription. But I'm telling you that the best prescription I can give you is the light on that little bay. You'll sleep the sleep of the just there and eat like an Irish hunter.'

When would she know the worst? He could be honest with her.

'There's no worst to know. There's nothing organically wrong with you. You're a perfectly healthy woman and all you need is a change – that's all, Miss Maitland. So wallow in your raspberries and cream and catch a brace of brown trout for me.'

'But I've never fished in my life.'

'Well, now's the time to begin. Liam Cassidy's the man to teach you.'

A week later she was in Ireland. After just over another week she was writing the first of her many letters to herself.

The little Cassidy Hotel had four front bow windows that stuck out from the whitewashed walls like pleasant rounded paunches. The small tributary of the Kenmare that came down from the hills behind seemed always to have a tender breath of mist on it in the early mornings and a rarefied scintillation of pure silver by noon.

From the very first day Dr O'Brien emerged and grew in stature as a prophet. The raspberries and cream were truly sumptuous, the trout noble in their butter, the sunsets brilliant as ripe apricots. Mrs Cassidy was a wide, comfortable cushion of a woman who talked in the dreamy brown accents of a summer bumble bee.

Her husband Liam looked like a bony, beery, mischievous jockey who had seen better days but still persisted in a fanciful belief that horses were more princely than men and that one day he would pick out a colt with solid gold hoofs and mother of pearl in its eyes. The twittering slyness in his own small brown eyes at first dismayed Miss Maitland. She was all too sure, when constantly he called her beautiful, that her leg was being pulled.

But soon it came to her that everything and everybody, in the Irish way, was beautiful. The word bestowed itself as naturally on things and people as the mist of early morning clothed the face of the stream, and the magenta and purple bells of fuchsia clothed every hedgerow. Even Dr O'Brien was beautiful.

'A beautiful man. A beautiful man. He was no more than sixteen when he first came here, all the way from Dublin, on his bone-shaker, with hardly the price of a fly in his pocket. Ah, a beautiful man.'

'Has he been back here lately?'

'Ah, he's in England now. He's in England now.' And the words might have been the beginning and the end of a funeral dirge.

The air was always so damply soft that Miss Maitland

took on the feeling, and even the appearance, of a well-fed, sleepy cat. She slept with undiminished peace at night and woke to eat prodigious breakfasts of Irish bacon and eggs and honey and brown loaves baked in a wood-fired oven.

Once or twice a day she went through the apprentice-ship of learning to cast a fly under the twittering and half-affectionate gaze of Liam Cassidy; until the day came, after a week, when she took her first brace of trout in trembling triumph back to the hotel.

It was also a triumph for the prophetic powers of Dr O'Brien. Vividly she remembered his words, '*Wallow in your raspberries and cream and catch a brace of trout for me,*' and it was almost as if he had actually willed her to do such things.

So strong were her feelings of both gratitude and triumph about all this that that evening she felt impelled to sit down and write to him: first to say how splendidly right he had been about everything, the raspberries and cream, the trout, the sunsets, the Cassidys, the soft sea air; then of how restored and relaxed she was; then of the triumph of the trout.

'*I must confess I felt like a child opening a Christmas stocking or something. I could have screamed when I hooked the first one. Well, anyway, I'm going to have them for supper tonight and just as a celebration I'm going to have half a bottle of white wine with them. And of course I shall drink your health, because if it hadn't been for you I wouldn't be here and in a way they're really your trout more than mine.*

'*Liam and Mrs Cassidy, by the way, send their best regards to you and only wish that you were here. Liam still* makes that nectar of a drink with honey and whiskey which he says you invented. It looks so innocuous and tastes so heavenly and then all of a sudden it hits you and you go all whoozy. I don't know if it's this that makes me sleep so well, but sleep I do – like a top.

'By the way, I've decided to let the office go hang and stay here for three weeks instead of two. I know you're awfully busy – I expect it's measles year or something and you're run off your feet – but it would be nice if you could drop me a line and include a word for the Cassidys. They sort of dote on you, you know. Anyway, I'm terribly grateful to you for the best prescription a patient ever had.

'Yours most sincerely, Meg Maitland.

'P.S. No doubt the "Meg" surprises you, but this is Liam's little joke. He wouldn't, in the name o' God, as he said, have a girl with a Welsh name learning to fish on an Irish river; so suddenly he christens me Meg. I must say I rather like it. It sort of fits the new me.'

After that, hopefully and then more and more eagerly, she waited for a reply; until it became, after a week, an obsession. Soon, she was sleeping badly again. Lying for long periods awake, she found herself composing the things she wanted Dr O'Brien to say to her. Mostly these first imaginary letters were merely formal and brief.

Then gradually they grew more vividly, intimately and optimistically longer. Finally she actually sat down and, for the first time, with a curiously combined feeling of guilt and excitement, wrote a letter to herself.

'*You'll understand how busy I am – yes, it's measles year – but I've just got time to snatch a moment to say it gives me a great deal of satisfaction to know that my prescription worked. I only wish I could come and share the trout and the sunsets with you, but until we get the measles thing beaten there isn't a hope. My love to the Cassidys, especially to Liam, the old rascal. So he still makes that devil's brew, does he? I might have known.*'

Then, after reading the letter through several times, she suddenly felt sharply vexed with herself and tore it up. It was really an extraordinarily silly thing to do, writing to oneself. You couldn't cheat like that.

Immediately, with the letter torn up, she was aware of feeling strangely cheated herself. It was rather like having a cup dashed from your lips at the moment of drinking. The anticipatory thrill of the moment was shattered, leaving a void.

She started to fill the void with new thoughts of Dr O'Brien. Soon it was remarkably easy to imagine that he was actually there at the little hotel. Soon she could see herself, mornings and evenings, fishing with him, walking the lanes between the dripping lush bells of fuchsia hedges, sipping Liam's devil's brew in the bar, even sharing a table and a bottle of wine with him over the evening trout. It was easiest of all, perhaps, to hear his voice talking to her in the deep immeasurable quietness of the remote sea soft air.

*   *   *

The result of all this was to throw her into a new state of sleepless conflict. By three o'clock one morning she had worked herself up into a torment of restless exhaustion, almost a fever, when some physical action and exercise seemed the only possible remedies to desperation. She dressed, went downstairs, let herself out of the hotel and started to walk.

A soft light drizzle was already falling. As it gradually increased she heard it plopping with big warm drops on to the water of the trout stream, on the surrounding mass of heavy summer leaves and on her own uplifted face.

'Oh, I wish to God you were here. I know you can't be but perhaps you could write, just once. Couldn't you? Just once. Please.'

When she at last went home, vowing in farewell her fervent intention of coming back next year, it was to take with her not only pots of honey and a bottle of Irish whiskey so that she could sometimes make Liam's devil's brew, but something of much more importance: several dozen sheets of the Cassidy Hotel notepaper.

Back at the office an astonished Mrs Braithwaite confessed herself slightly bowled over by a transformed, rejuvenated Miss Maitland.

'Well, if that's what Ireland can do for you I'm not sure I won't give it a go myself. Is it the whiskey, the blarney or something in the air?'

'The air is wonderful.'

'By the look of you I'd say it was miraculous. Make any friends?'

'Liam and Mrs Cassidy – they keep the hotel. Otherwise—'

'Come clean.'

Miss Maitland smiled in a secretive sort of way. 'Well, you could sort of say I made *a* friend . . . '

'I see, I see, I see. Tell me.'

'There isn't much to tell. It's strictly friendship. Well, so far—'

'Some wild Irish boyo sweeping you off your feet?'

'Oh, nothing like that. He's Irish, yes, but very quiet. He's a doctor.'

Mrs Braithwaite was moved through mere astonishment to a display of great relish and satisfaction. It was marvellous to see the change in Miss Maitland, the transformation. She looked another woman. It was quite wonderful what love could do.

'I didn't say anything about love.'

It was now Mrs Braithwaite's turn to laugh. 'My foot. Naturally. Just as if I was born yesterday.'

'Friendship can do a lot too.'

Friendship was all right, Mrs Braithwaite said, but she didn't think a lot of it from a distance. You couldn't warm it up very much with Ireland all that far away. When did she hope to see him again?

'Oh soon. I'll probably fly over for a long weekend in September. In the meantime he'll be writing. Oh, by the way, I learned to fish.'

'So,' Mrs Braithwaite said, 'it would seem.'

From then until September – when she was to fly back

for the promised long weekend at the Cassidy Hotel –
Miss Maitland typed one letter a week to herself as from
Dr O'Brien, on the Cassidy Hotel notepaper. As appetite
grows on what it feeds on, in the same way the hallucination that the letters were in fact from Dr O'Brien profoundly increased with every letter. Their warmth,
intimacy and sheer affection increased profoundly too.

Consistently, from the first, she wrote them every Saturday. This was in order that they should arrive on Monday
morning; so that she could be sure that each week would
begin with excitement, as it were with a fresh blossoming.

After some weeks Mrs Braithwaite was moved to
remark one Monday morning at the office: 'I've spoken
to you twice and you haven't answered. Have you
spotted a flying saucer in our damp August clouds or
what?'

'Sorry. I was a long way away.'

'Unless my eyes deceive me we've come a long way
from just friendship.'

'I had a wonderful letter today.'

Mrs Braithwaite said nothing. After a few moments
Miss Maitland took the letter from her handbag. 'I'd let
you read it if you'd care to. Well, part of it anyway—'

'Oh no. I don't want to pry into—'

'It's perfectly all right. I'd like you to. Or anyway just
the first and the last paragraphs.'

Miss Maitland unfolded the letter and gave it to Mrs

Braithwaite, who glanced at it before starting to read. 'Oh, I see he writes from the hotel.'

'Yes. He's staying there until he can find a house.'

' "*My dear Meg*," ' Mrs Braithwaite read. 'Who on earth is Meg?'

'That's me. That's his sort of pet name for me. He said he rather hated the name Gladys and he couldn't have a girl with a name like that fishing on an Irish river, so he started to call me Meg. I think it rather suits me. It sort of makes me feel a new person.'

Without answering, Mrs Braithwaite read on: ' "*I went down to the estuary today and took a boat. It was quite warm, no wind at all, and a lot of people were bathing on one of the little beaches. I kept thinking all the time of you and how we ought to go down there and bathe too when you come over next time. So don't forget – bring your swimsuit. It's a perfectly heavenly spot and I just longed for you to be there today.*" '

Finally, Mrs Braithwaite read the last paragraph. ' "*I've actually added up the number of days until you come over in September. I don't know if you know how I feel – I'm not sure if it's agonizing or a thrill, waiting that long. Perhaps you feel the same? Sometimes it seems the time will never pass. Do you feel that way? Anyway I'll be patient – or try anyway. You'll be here one day, and in the meantime I'll think about you every working minute. With all my love – Sean.*" '

'What an awfully nice letter,' Mrs Braithwaite said. 'It's somehow so simple and so genuine.'

'That's him, you see.'

After this, Miss Maitland no longer felt inferior to Mrs Braithwaite. She too, she told herself over and over again, had her own source of radiance.

This radiance remained with her throughout the next two months. A long September weekend at the Cassidy Hotel merely served to increase it. During the five days she was there a soft warm Atlantic rain fell most of the time. Low slate-blue clouds clothed the mountains like turgid smoke. The little trout stream boiled over its banks, so that there was no fishing. Instead she walked for hours, mackintosh-clad, happy in the illusion that Dr O'Brien walked with her.

Out of all that weekend one incident alone stood out from the uneventful, damp, placid daily routine. Late one afternoon the rain at last ceased, a great apricot gap opened up in the Atlantic curtain of cloud in the west; and she went out into the back garden of the hotel to find Liam Cassidy about to saw logs.

She started to chat. Then after a few moments she became aware of a small tree just behind him. Its every head of white blossom dripped with rain. What tree was this? she said.

'That's the strawberry tree, Meg. The arbutus. Have you never heard of the song – *My love is like an arbutus?*'

She had never heard of the tree or the song, but from that moment on she was unable to forget either. Soon, she began to sign the letters from Dr O'Brien: *your beloved arbutus.*

She went through another eighteen months and three visits to the Cassidy Hotel in perfect happiness: untroubled, painless, sleeping well. All the time the letters from Dr O'Brien, the beloved arbutus, piled up, more real than reality.

This might have gone on happily and indefinitely if it hadn't been for a remark of Mrs Braithwaite's. 'I wanted to ask you . . . What do they charge at your Irish hotel?'

'Charge? What makes you ask?'

'We thought we'd spend Easter over there. Take the car and tour round a bit. It sounds so marvellous.'

Miss Maitland, gripped in cold confusion, found her tongue frozen.

'Jack adores fishing and perhaps we could meet this boy friend of yours.'

A sudden hot rush of emotion unfroze Miss Maitland's tongue, so that she blurted out: 'Oh, I don't think it's for you. It's far too simple. It isn't you at all. No, I don't think you'd like it, not at all.'

'The simpler it is, the better Jack likes it. Don't worry!'

From that moment the old afflictions began to return: the sleeplessness, the nausea, the pain, the inability to eat, the melancholic headaches. As the time drew nearer for the Braithwaites to depart for Ireland, Miss Maitland was in deeper and deeper distress.

At last she telephoned Dr O'Brien. 'I was wondering if I might have more sleeping tablets, Doctor . . . '

'Of course. Could you call for the prescription? I'll leave it inside the window at the front of the surgery.'

'Thank you very much, Doctor.'

The effect on her of this short simple conversation was nothing less than shattering. The reality of the actual sound of the doctor's voice threw into harsh relief all the unreality of the letters, the absurdity of love that never existed, the painful myth of the beloved arbutus.

Soon Mrs Braithwaite and her husband departed, Mrs Braithwaite with the cheerful words: 'Jack's taking his movie camera. We'll get yards of film of your boy friend and then you can wallow in it when we get back.'

She began to wallow, instead, in nothing but a well of self-persecution. Alone in the bedsitter, on an evening of heavy rain, she sat for hours staring starkly at the wall, trying to face the thought of the Braithwaites' return. It seemed to her that the rain outside was black. The April evening sky, prematurely nearly dark, had about it a greenish unreality.

At last the desire to speak once again to Dr O'Brien was too much for her. In desperation she dialled his number. 'Might I possibly speak to Dr O'Brien please?'

'I'm sorry, he's away on holiday.'

'Oh God!'

'What . . ? I beg your pardon?'

'Oh, nothing. Has he gone over to Ireland?'

'No. To the Austrian Tyrol. He will be away for about three weeks.'

'I see. Thank you.'

In the ensuing silence she sat down and wrote the last of her letters to herself. Having written it, she then tore it up. Then she mixed herself a long strong tumbler of Liam's devil's brew. Then she emptied the entire contents of the bottle of sleeping tablets into the palm of her hand and slowly, one by one, began to swallow them, washing them down with first one tumbler of whiskey and then another; then she lay down on the bed and shut her eyes.

After only a few seconds she got up again and in her own handwriting wrote a short farewell note.

'*Goodbye*,' it said simply, '*my beloved arbutus.*'

The Lap of Luxury

'STILL carry your rabbit's foot? I do. Never be without it. Sort of St Christopher.'

They were driving south through France, Roger Stiles and Maxie Forbes, in Maxie's two-seater open job that constantly sounded like a broken down lathe and some venerable wind instrument somehow played from the wrong end. It was Maxie, a big, burly, rather swaggering type, who was driving and it was he too who carried the rabbit's foot. The war had been over thirteen months.

Back in 1940, during that period known as the phoney war, both had been fighter pilots, in the same squadron, flying over France. Both had been shot down within forty-eight hours of each other, Roger largely because he lost his way; both had found themselves in the same prisoner-of-war camp in Germany. Maxie was the type of man who, in civil life, makes coarse jokes at weddings, sends even coarser telegrams to the bride and bridegroom and ends the wedding day by tying old buckets, salmon tins and enamel chamber pots to the back of the happy couple's car, for ever laughing like a bellowing bull at each successive tasteless joke.

Such characters, abruptly confined to prison walls, find themselves a new identity. They grow up, revealing themselves to be men of resource and resolution, with minds of steel, determined almost with ferocity not to be bullied either by camp commandants or guards, to assert the rights of prisoners according to the Geneva convention and to employ every possible subterfuge to escape. No longer puerile jokers, they become men of utterly new stature, inspirational leaders of men.

Roger Stiles could scarcely have been more different. His attitude in prison became that of a quiet, caged rabbit, lost for the most part in meditation. Good looking, blue-eyed, flaxen haired, he couldn't have looked more English, more of a gentleman. Coarse jokes, at weddings or elsewhere, occupied no place in his repertoire. He was exactly the incongruous type who seems to be the complete reverse of men of action until suddenly war blows up in their faces and they too are revealed, in their own own way, to be men of steel.

In this way, as so often happens with opposites, the two men became close friends. Maxie, the positive, fused with Roger, the apparent negative, to make friendship an harmonious entity. Roger never thought of escape; Maxie worked at it, day in, day out, night and day, as a beaver works to build its dam, never resting until the ultimate structure has been achieved. One of Maxie's escape schemes was that Roger, looking so much the Nordic type, should dress as a girl, take part in a theatrical sketch and somehow get spirited away under the floorboards of the stage. All appeared to be going well until Maxie accidentally trod on a sleeping cat.

Maxie had countless other schemes, some ingenious, some decidedly not, all beset with failure. Then he made the discovery that although it was immensely difficult to escape from within the compound it was comparatively easy to do so from any of the working parties sent out into the country. His chief need to set him and Roger on this particular path was a couple of pairs of trousers that looked both peasant-like and agricultural and a pair of shirts to match. The trousers were made eventually from old potato sacks and the shirts from strips of bed ticking.

In due course, in the fading light of a September afternoon, the two men slipped the working party, hid for a time in a birch wood and then, with the fall of darkness, began walking. 'Piece o' cake,' Maxie kept saying as they strode the moonless miles, 'piece o' bloody cake'. A piece of cake it was until, some ten miles further on, Roger paused to make water by a tree. The tree, by a stroke of sad misfortune, turned out to be a German sentry.

Maxie walked on.

Now, together again, they were beginning a sentimental journey. It was Maxie's idea. His purpose was to take Roger over the route that he, Maxie, had traced to the Swiss border: no ordinary route this but one, if Maxie was to be believed, embellished every few miles with Rabelaisian adventure. The purveyor of coarse meat, laughing like a bull, was once again the life and soul of his own party. The account of conferring certain physical favours on a farmer's wife was succeeded by conferring similar favours on the two daughters of a Mayor. It was wonderful, Maxie would have Roger know, what miracles could be accomplished in beds, woods and fields of corn. 'Can't go wrong, old Boy, if you keep your hand on your rabbit's foot, or theirs.'

As they drove on Roger Stiles found himself more and more enmeshed in a shroud of depression. The French countryside had begun to fill him with boredom. He found himself staring soporifically at the map on his knees. And suddenly it was the map that offered a key of escape from Maxie's coarser world.

'I suppose you know, Maxie, that we're on the wrong road.'

'Hell! How come?'

'We're supposed to be heading for Pontalier. Right?'

'Right.'

'Well, this doesn't happen to be the road to Pontalier.'

'Don't talk cock. I saw the sign to Pontalier only a couple of kilometres back.'

'What you saw,' Roger said, 'was a sign to Pontaillier. Not Pontalier.'

'Then why the hell didn't you say so. You're supposed to be reading the bloody map.'

'Sorry. I was listening to the gospel according to St Maxie.'

The air was both chill and acid. For some three or four kilometres neither man spoke a word. Then Maxie growled:

'And how far is this pissing Pont-something-or-other from Pontalier.'

'Probably a matter of a hundred kilometres.'

'For Jesus! – no wonder you got lost over France that day if that's the best you can do in the way of navigation.'

'One more remark like that and I'll get out and walk.'

'Suit your bloody self. Walk if that's what you want. The roads are free.'

'That's exactly what I want. Stop the car.'

With a gesture as if he were jumping on some offensive animal Maxie put on the brakes. The machine that sounded like a cross between a rusty lathe and an ancient wind instrument blown from the wrong end shrieked to a halt.

Roger Stiles leaned backward and seized his suitcase from the back of the car and then got out of the car and stood in the road.

With neither word nor gesture of farewell Maxie, no longer looking the part of joker, slammed in the clutch and drove furiously away.

The hot mid afternoon sky was like a shimmering steel scythe. Roger Stiles' fingers, first of the right hand, then the left, were as sticky as melted butter. Always the road ahead was dead straight and, again like a sharpened scythe, severed the far quivering horizon. Scorched to the colour of straw, the roadsides were as hard on the eyes as burnt cinder tracks.

Roger Stiles' mind offered a surface no less dead. Having left the map in the car he hadn't the remotest idea of where he was or, worse still, where he was going. His sudden explosion of temper had left him alternately seething and sick. When a coherent thought rose to the surface of his mind it was always the same. This, he would tell himself, might well have been his lot, back in 1940, if he hadn't mistaken a man for a tree.

Presently the countryside grew hillier. Its contours were like the carcases of dead animals under the blistering sun. A kestrel, hovering over a shallow basin shut in by withered bracken, looked for all the world like some nervous, shimmering slice of heat haze.

The only other sign of life was a stone farmhouse in the middle distance, at the end of a dusty white track, where a few black hens, themselves looking as if scorched, pecked at a heap of straw. By now his thirst was of such excruciating pain that he was just about to succumb to the impulse of asking for water at the farmhouse when the double hoot of a car horn made him half turn his head.

A black Citroen passed him, continued for forty or fifty yards along the road and then stopped. An impulse to run after it merely brought home to him the fact that his legs, like his fingers, were made of butter too.

When at last he caught up with the car the hatless head of a woman, fiftyish, blonde, her arms bare to the shoulders, was leaning out of the window. She spoke in French.

Had he far to go? Did he desire a lift? She herself was going about twenty kilometres farther on.

His fatigued mind had gone so far in weariness that his answering few words of French melted too. He begged to know if she spoke English.

'But yes. Certainly. Are things all right with you? It is very hot. You look tired.'

'I – I –'

'You had better get into the car.'

A series of half conscious movements resulted in his sitting, like a collapsed sack, in the seat next to the driver. He was vaguely aware of his suitcase being taken from him and put into the back seat of the car. An involuntary gasp for air, somewhere between a deep sigh and a stifled groan, made her say:

'This heat is killing. Have you come far?'

'You haven't, I suppose, something to drink?'

'I always carry a flask of cognac.'

A gulp of cognac convinced him that the afternoon had distilled itself into liquid fire.

'Take another drink. It is good cognac. It can do you no harm.'

He drank again. Fire scoured his belly and his mind swayed. He discovered now that his buttery fingers were trembling. A moment or two later she discovered it too and suddenly seized both his hands in hers and gripped them with great firmness.

'Are things all right? You could have heatstroke, walking in this sun without a hat. You should know that, shouldn't you?'

'Yes. But I left my brains at home.'

'Take one more drink.'

He drank again from the cognac, still dazed, her hands still holding his.

'Better?'

Yes, he said, he felt better.

'You wish we should drive on?'

'Please. Yes. I will be all right now.'

She had sense enough not to speak again for another five kilometres or so. She also had sense enough to drive slowly, so that the car was almost silent. By now his brain had begun to work with some coherence and it was he in fact who was the first to speak.

'How far is the nearest town? I should really find myself a hotel.'

'Here there are not many towns. Or hotels. It is all rather isolated. Sometimes I call it Indian country.'

'Perhaps I could get a train?'

'Well, we shall see about that.' She turned and gave him a steady, searching look. 'Why don't you close your eyes for a few moments? It will rest you. It will do you good.'

The closing of his eyes was as involuntary as his earlier gasp for air had been. Within a few seconds weariness and cognac together had put him into a deep-breathing coma from which he woke, how long later he never knew, to realize that the car was travelling, as he thought, through a tunnel. This tunnel, he presently realized, was a shadowy avenue of chestnut trees.

The car stopped. A house of considerable size, embellished with turrets and towers so typical of French country châteaux, stood beyond the end of the avenue.

'This, if you wish, is your hotel.'

'Oh! but I couldn't impose—'

'At least you can rest for a while.'

She took his suitcase from the back of the car, opened the door for him to get out and then started to walk to the house. He followed. By now his senses had so far recovered that he saw that her legs were refined, her figure upright and rather full at the top.

He was however still too dazed to realize that so far everything had been done at her instigation. Now he had a further example of her insistence.

'I think you should take a bath and then lie down for a while. Then I will make iced coffee.'

He started to say something about telephoning for a taxi and then catching a train when she cut him short with some abruptness by saying:

'Why do you speak of trains? Have you an appointment somewhere?'

'No.'

'Very well. What does one of your English poets say? "Everything comes to him who waits." '

'True.'

'Then you should wait. It will be good for you.'

He duly went upstairs and bathed, luxuriating in tepid, fragrant water, some of his weariness draining away. When he went downstairs again he found her listening to a movement of a Brahms' symphony on a gramophone. Seeing him arrive she shut it off, greeting him with the most enchanting of smiles.

'Ah! that is better. Now you look like a new boy.'

He noted the word boy. He noted too that she had changed her dress and was now wearing one of the lightest yellow material, rather low-cut at the neck and with neither embellishments nor pattern. The effect was to make her look much younger. Whereas in the afternoon, in the oppressive heat of the day, she had seemed to him a woman of fifty or more she now looked no more than forty.

'You see, I told you a little relaxation would be good for you. Would you like iced coffee or perhaps a little cold wine?'

He confessed he preferred wine and she said: 'Good. I'm inclined to agree with you. I will ring for Anne Marie.'

There presently came into the room a rather dumpy woman wearing one of those dainty white lace caps that are survivals from another era. She in fact actually curtsied with gentle restraint as her mistress gave her order.

When she had departed he found himself looking out of the window at the garden beyond. It was rectangular in shape, enclosed by limestone walls capped by orange tiles. He could see golden balloons of ripe melons growing by a path and then, on the walls, scarlet-crimson peaches.

'I see you are looking at the garden. Please don't. My gardener died two weeks ago and here it is imposs-ible, impossible, impossible to get another to replace him. Do you like gardens?'

'I quite often help my father in his from time to time.'

'I only wish you could help in mine.'

A few moments later Anne Marie came back with a tray of glasses, a bowl of sweet biscuits and a bottle of wine. The wine had already been uncorked and she poured out a small measure for her mistress to taste.

'*Excellent. Merci.*'

The wine as it filled the two glasses was of a clear deep tan-rose. Its coldness misted the sides of the glasses.

'Ah! *rosé*,' he said. '*Pelure d'oignon* perhaps. From here?'

'Not from here. Not *pelure d'oignon*. No, it is from Arbois. I hope you will find it good.'

He drank and raised his glass to her. In return she gave him the frankest and most charming of smiles.

'It *is* good. In fact marvellous.'

'I am pleased you like it. Well, we celebrate your arrival here.'

He drank again, rolling the cold wine round on his tongue. 'As you said, everything comes to him who waits.'

'Yes. And perhaps he who waits longest receives more of everything. Tell me about yourself. How did you come to be walking along that road? Are you *en vacances?*'

'In a way, yes. In a way, no. It was the beginning of a sentimental journey.' He proceeded to explain, briefly, about Maxie and himself. For some reason it all sounded improbably ludicrous.

'It was all too, too stupid. The trouble was we were trying to recapture something that was never there.'

'In other words "never go back".'

'Exactly.'

She poured more wine, stared thoughtfully for some moments at her glass and then said:

'My husband was in the French Air Force. He too was taken prisoner. I never saw him again.'

'Did he try to escape?'

'It was for that reason they shot him.'

Once again she drank and now, after gazing into her glass, abruptly changed the subject.

'Why are you so anxious to get a train? Must you go

back to England to work? Have you a wife?'

He confessed he had neither a job nor a wife.

'Nor a reason.'

No, he had to confess, nor a reason.

'Why don't you stay here for a few days? There is room. Anne Marie is a divine cook. There is wine. And if you get bored you can help me pick peaches.'

'You have a way of making things sound idyllic.'

'Any why not? Why rush? What is wrong with letting the world go by?'

They sat drinking wine for another hour or more, a second bottle following the first. The wine was cold and light on the tongue and easy on the head and limbs. The restoration of his spirit presently became so complete that he suddenly leaned forward, put a hand on one of her knees, looked straight at her eyes and said:

'I don't even know your name. But I just feel I must thank you for all you have done for me today. I was ready to jump into the nearest lake – if there had been a lake.'

'It is I who should thank you. After all I am quite alone here except for Anne Marie. It is good to have someone to talk to. My name is Louise.'

It was nearly midnight before the excellence of Anne Marie's dinner, more wine and a glass or two of Armagnac began to sweep him quietly but surely towards sleepiness.

'You must sleep late tomorrow. If you need coffee or anything just ring the bell in your room and Anne Marie will bring it up.'

They parted with a brief good night. She extended her

hand and he shook it gently. Her eyes engaged him in a slow smile of enchantment in which there might have been the subtlest hint of invitation.

'Good-night. Sleep well.'

'And you. Sleep well. *Dormez bien.* Good-night.'

He went upstairs. Before getting into bed he stood at the window and took a last look at the garden. A faint moon was setting, giving just enough light for him to detect odd objects here and there.

Suddenly he saw her walking slowly along a path. Her yellow dress, bathed in the faint moonlight, had something both ethereal and unreal about it. The air contained no breath of wind and along the path the melons shone golden, like the moon's reflections.

He found it impossible to believe that it was past midday before he woke. He shaved, dressed himself, decided to forget about coffee and went downstairs. Neither Anne Marie nor Louise seemed to be in the house and he wandered into the garden, where the sun was already beating down with the ferocity of a torch.

He finally detected the two women over on the far side of the garden, picking peaches from a wall.

'We have so many peaches that Anne Marie is going to pickle some. Would you like breakfast?'

'Thanks. I don't think so. I'll settle for a peach.'

'What better? They are really superb. I hope you slept well?'

'I spent the night in another world.'

It wasn't long before they were sitting in the house, again drinking the cold, fresh *Rosé d'Arbois*. Today she was wearing a simple blue skirt with an open-neck almost transparent blouse that made her look younger than ever. Her constant smile of enchantment captivated him even more than it had done the day before and soon he found himself slipping into the semi-coma of a daylight dream.

'It's nice to see you relaxing. That's all you should do. It's good for you.'

For several days after this he obeyed her constant injunction to sleep late, take it easy and let the world go by. He luxuriated in long indolent afternoons made all the drowsier by wine. From time to time a brief thought of Maxie crossed his mind, only to be flicked away like a fly on a window pane.

One morning, after about a week of this, he began to feel uncommonly restless. Instead of sleeping late he was downstairs before nine, to discover her, still in a dressing gown, having her *café complet* on the terrace in front of the house. Her pleasure at seeing him so early was expressed in a mock concern that she hoped he wasn't getting into bad habits.

As she poured his coffee he sat looking at the hills, not yet molten in the blistering sun as they would be by afternoon but a soft diaphanous grey that made them, for some reason, seem unusually near. And as he sat watching them he found himself assailed by an uneasy recollection of the prison camp in Germany. The hills also seemed to be imprisoning him. He was locked in. What was worse was a growing impression that he was not only locked in but that he would never get out. As in the prison camp he suddenly longed, almost painfully, to escape.

'Well, I think this is the day,' he said.

'Day? What day? The day for what?'

'The day to shake myself out of myself and get going.'

'For what reason? You have no job. You have no wife—'

'And, you forget, no money.'

'I have money.'

'I don't sponge on my friends.'

The hardening look on her face reproached him far more than any chorus of words could have done. In fact she made no attempt to speak again, the tension in the air all the time growing to such a pitch that finally he had to break the silence by saying:

'Yes, if you'll excuse me, I'll go and pack.'

She had no word to offer about this and he went upstairs. He had been sorting out his few belongings for something like five minutes when he heard a tap on the bedroom door and she came in.

'I came to apologise for what I said about money.'

'It's I who should apologise.'

'No, no. But I *have* money. Lots. My husband's family were car manufacturers. He left oceans of shares.'

'You see, I don't need money. I have enough to get back.'

'I was very, very tactless. I can never forgive myself for that.' .

To his infinite astonishment he realized that she was on the verge of tears. He took both her hands in his,

D

looked straight at her tear-wet eyes and said:

'But you're crying. It surely wasn't as tactless as all that.'

In answer she released her hands and held his face in them. The gesture was so abrupt that the neck of her dressing gown fell apart, revealing her night-dress underneath. A moment later she started kissing him. The desperate nature of this took him so much by surprise that he was momentarily unprepared for another gesture from her. She seized his hands and held them against her breasts.

'Lie on the bed with me,' she said. 'I will lock the door.'

Some long time later, how long he hadn't the capacity to calculate, she gave a long exultant sigh, pressing her breasts against him.

'Have you loved many women?'

'Very few.'

'The fortunate few. The very fortunate few.'

'Does that mean you want me to love you again?'

'Of course. Naturally. Can you think of anything lovelier?'

As summer cooled into autumn and then autumn to the edge of winter he found that they spoke to each other more and more in French. Often she praised his French. He was beginning to speak it well. His accent was good. She felt it brought them closer together.

For him it forged a new sort of bondage. The sense of

imprisonment was all the stronger but now there was no thought of escape. Life was now a Lotus Land of mornings in the garden, half-playing, half-working at trivial tasks, long wine-coloured afternoons and evenings of music prolonged by wine.

'It's beginning to get cold. We should go into Besançon and get you a good big warm overcoat.'

'Do you get snow here?'

'Oh! the Juras will be covered in snow.'

The arrival of the first snow, late in November, was another instrument of bondage. Now he scarcely ever left the house. The habit of sleeping late renewed itself with consummate ease. Now that snow covered the ground such little initiative as he had once had dissipated itself altogether and work in the garden came at last to a standstill. He found himself drinking more and more heavily and in consequence putting on weight. His mind began to feel fatty too.

Was he happy? she would ask him from time to time.

Yes, he would say. A more truthful answer would have been that he was not happy but possessed. The fact that he was a mere possession of hers wasn't to be brought home to him for some long time yet, but meanwhile who was he to argue against the life she had chosen for him to lead?

Spring started at last to melt the snows. Fragile, magic carpets of crocus appeared, white and mauve and gold.

'We should take the car one afternoon and drive up into the Juras and walk in the woods and see the wild flowers.'

'Is it necessary?'

'It will do you good.'

'I don't think I want to be done good to.'

'Funny boy. You make me laugh sometimes.'

There were times when he, by contrast, felt very far from laughing. Sometimes in the mornings, after some heavier session of wine and cognac, he would stand in front of the bathroom mirror and try to address himself dispassionately.

'You degenerate-looking sod. She's right. You should take a walk in the woods sometimes. Bloody bloated, that's what you look.'

From time to time he thought of England, of his mother and father. It was the time of year when his father would be potting up his chrysanthemums. He wondered what his parents' thoughts were and told himself that he ought to write to them.

What would he say? 'I am in prison. On Easy Street. Lap of luxury. Marvellous food and wine. Nothing to do. Beautiful country. Plenty of money. Passionate woman. What more can a man ask than that?'

A conscience stifled by wine and indolence relieved him of the task of writing even a single letter. It was, as Louise so often said, so much simpler to let the world go by.

One warm spring day Louise drove home from the nearest town and presented him with a green baize apron.

'And what the devil is this for?'

'It's for you, the gardener. Now you can really look the part.'

'You're damn right I can.'

After putting on the apron he did in fact look the part. 'Bloody hired servant,' he told himself, 'that's what I look like. Perhaps that's what I am.'

Hired? Possessed? In bondage, out of bondage? Did it matter? The days were rapidly growing warmer. There were little downy green peaches on the garden walls.

A few mornings later she met him in the garden, along the path where big orange-yellow melon flowers were already flaunting themselves wide open in the sun.

'Would you like a nice, pleasant, easy task for today?'

'And what would that be?'

'The peaches need thinning. Unless we do that the fruit will be too small. It's very easy. You can take your time.'

He put on his green apron and turned his attention to the peaches while she went back into the house. It was exactly as she had said: a pleasant, unarduous task. The sun was not yet torrid although the hills, seeming to brood near again, held promise of heat for the afternoon.

He had been working at the peaches for an hour or so when he was aware of a figure walking towards him along the path by the wall: a tallish, good looking man of fifty or so in a light-weight cream suit, his face deep bronze under his still black hair.

'Ah, I am looking for madame. She is here?'

Caught unawares and momentarily forgetting himself he replied in English.

'I think she is in the house.'

'In that case I will go and search for her. You are English?'

'Yes.'

'Ah, madame is lucky to have an English gardener. I have always heard how good the English are at gardens. Have you been with her long? I have been away in Martinique for a year. Ah! there is madame now. Louise!'

Louise was coming up the path that ran alongside the melon flowers. Seeing her visitor she gave an excited exclamation, 'Pierre! Oh! Pierre,' threw her hands high and wide in the air and started running. Her visitor started running too and a moment or two later they met by the melon flowers, locked in embrace, she kissing him openly on the lips as she might have kissed some long-lost lover.

Oblivious of Roger Stiles she and Pierre joined arms, both laughing with excitement, and then turned and went into the house. Even as they disappeared he could still hear their ringing, excited laughter.

For some time he stood by the peach wall without moving, simply staring at three or four downy immature green peaches lying in the palm of his hand. When he finally did move and look up it was to be assailed once again by the imprisoning effect of the brooding hills.

In an effort to rid himself of the stifling notion of being locked in he walked along the path to where the wall ended. There he stopped and locked his hands together and held them against the top of the wall. They were trembling violently, so much so that he could no longer hold the little peaches and let them fall to the ground.

In a daze through which he could scarcely see the imprisoning hills he started talking to himself.

'What's that damn poem? No, not the one about

everything comes to him who waits. Not that one. No, another. I learnt it at school. Can't remember who wrote it now. "Stone walls do not a prison make". Stone walls – stone walls – do not a prison—'

Loss of Pride

MY uncle Silas, all his life, was very fond of a baked potato. Whenever I walked over to see him on cold midwinter nights, when roadsides were crisp and white with hoarfrost and you could hear cold owl-cry haunting the woods, his first words were almost always: 'You git the taters, boy, while I git the wine.'

He was always very particular, I noticed, about how the potatoes were cooked. 'Course they're better in a twitch fire,' he often said, 'when it's died down a bit and you can poke 'em into that hot ash. You git that burnt taste in 'em then and it teks a bit o' beatin.'

But in the absence of twitch fires he did the next best thing. At the side of his kitchen fireplace there used to be one of those big baking ovens, large enough to hold a side of mutton, where in the old days faggots were lit for baking bread. When the fired faggots had died down the big pink-and-white kidney potatoes, pricked all over with a fork, went into the bed of ash and soon the little kitchen was sweet and warm with the smell of their cooking.

'Ever tell you about Pouchy Reeves and the baked taters? Bin a minute – very like I never did. The smell on 'em allus brings it back.'

In winter time we almost always drank elderberry wine, sometimes slightly mulled if the nights were very cold, and it was generally at about the third or fourth glass that some reminiscence, far out of the past, began.

I said I didn't think he had; nor, I thought, had I ever heard of Pouchy.

'Shoemekker. Hand-craft. Bit of a dab hand, I'll grant him that. But knowed it – bit of a toff in a way, what shoemekkers used to call notch-above-a-tapper. Very cocky. Fancy westkits and walking sticks and big button-holes of a Sunday. Too high and mighty for the rest of us chaps.'

Here he licked a drop of wine from his lips with what I thought was no innocent relish and I proceeded to remark that it wouldn't have surprised me at all to hear that Pouchy, with such a splendid array of attractions and accomplishments, was also a great one with women.

'Never 'eerd nothing else. Wimmin mornin', noon and night. He wur a-gittin' on 'em into hayfields and stackyards and straw-barns and stables and I don't know wheer so fast you'd a thought he never had a minute fer shoemekking left. Young and old. Let 'em all come. Used to reckon he had two sisters in the same bed one turn over at the old mill-house at Shelton Cross.'

I at once remarked that this seemed to be a matter of very serious rivalry and in return he gave me a look, over the top of his wine-glass, that was almost pious in the bland severity of its rebuke.

'Now, hold hard. I've had a few gals in me time, one way an' another, but like I allus tell you – I wur never arter *them*, they wur allus arter *me*.'

'A very subtle difference.'

He said never mind about a very subtle difference, but when you got a man boasting he had two gals in bed at the same time and another up in the church belfry while the Sunday evening service was on and another in one corner of a wheatfield while her husband was mowing and bonding in another then you started to wonder.

'Another thing. Like I say, I've had a gal or two in me time and some fair samples among 'em too but I never done no poachin'. But Pouchy – he wur different. He liked nickin' on 'em from other chaps. It wur more fun.'

He then went on to ask me if I knew *The Swan with Two Necks* at Nenweald and the two old tits who kept it? When I said I did he said:

'Never think they was sisters, would you? Nell, she's like a damn great bean-pole and arms like a man. Lucy looks like a bit dropped off her, a real dillin. Course they're gittin' on a bit now but in my day Nell'd chook a man outa the bar as easy as spit in your eye. I seed her chook a man named Butch Waters out once, big labourin' man, fists like legs o' mutton. He never ony bounced once but it wur enough. He wur out cold as a gravestone fer a night and a day.'

After what was really an uncommonly long speech for him he took a good long draught of elderberry, refilled the glasses, wiped his mouth on the back of his hand and then opened the oven door to see how the baked potatoes were coming on. A hot delicious fragrance floated through the open oven door and he gave a great smacking sniff at it and then pressed first one potato and then another with his thumb.

'Give 'em another ten minutes. Git the butter and the salt, boy, then we'll be ready for 'em. Plenty o' butter.'

And what, I now wanted to know, having found the salt cellar and a big brown crock of butter, had the old tits to do with Pouchy?

'Well, they wad'n old then. I'm talkin' abut fifty year back. Very like more. In them days Lucy wur an uncommon good-lookin' gal, but freckly, like a thrush's egg.'

I here murmured that I supposed in consequence Pouchy was after her but he merely gave me another look of rather sharp reproof and said:

'I'm comin' to that if you'll let me breathe. You will git so fur ahead on me. No, she wur a-courtin' at the time.'

He laughed briefly, his old voice cracking, and took another sharp swig of wine.

'Well, you could call it courtin', in a way. This goodly chap Will Croome was arter 'er. Well, I say arter 'er. All he done wur to sit all night in the bar and just stare at 'er over 'is beer. Nice enough chap, but onaccountable shy. Bit on the deaf side, too.'

It was about this time, he went on, that Nell slipped on a patch of ice in the pub-yard and fell and broke her leg. It was mighty cold that winter: ten weeks of frost. You could put your skates on in the house and skate all the way through the frozen streets to the river. That was frozen solid too.

'Well, about that time there wur allus me and Tupman

Sanders and Olly Sharman and Ponto Pack and Gunner Jarvis in the *Swan* of a night and o' course this goodly Will Croome staring at Lucy.'

And then, no sooner had Nell been taken off to hospital, than Pouchy began to come in.

'Taters ready yit? Me belly's rollin' round. Give 'em another five minutes. I like 'em a bit black outside. Yis, Pouchy started to come in. Belch-guts. Mister High-and-Mighty. Notch above a tapper.'

'After the girl?'

'Well, at fust it wad'n so much that. It wur the way he kept on a-tauntin' and a-teasin' Will. Never give 'im no peace. Allus on at 'im. Nasty bits outa the side of 'is mouth. You know – "I see we got Will the Lady Killer in again tonight. Fast worker, Will. Moves like a whippet. Brought your salt with you tonight, Will boy? That's how you catch birds, Will – puttin' salt on their tails." It made it wuss because most o' the time Will couldn't hear.'

It would never have happened, he went on to say, if Nell had been there. You wouldn't have got away with that lark if Nell had been behind the bar. She'd have had you by the scruff of your neck and breeches and you'd have been out on your arse in one bounce if you tried that kind of caper.

'Better git the taters out, boy. Afore me belly drops out.'

While I was getting the potatoes out of the oven and finding plates for them and putting the salt and butter handy on the kitchen table he reminded me that all this was in the days before the *Swan* burnt down. It was the old *Swan* then, stone and thatched, and along one side of it was the big covered way for coaches. Every Saturday night, in winter, a man named Sprivvy Litchfield came and stood in there with his old hot potato oven, with a paraffin flare on top.

'We'd nip out and git half a dozen and eat 'em with the beer. Very good too, they wur. No better's these tonight, though.'

The potatoes, scalding hot and floury and drenched in butter, were too much for my tongue but Silas simply forked them into his ripe old mouth with never a cooling breath and as if they were nothing but luke-warm custard. He crackled at the dark burnt skin too and it struck me that it was just like the skin of his own gnarled earth-brown hands.

'Well, it got wusser and wusser, this 'ere teasin' an' tauntin'. I could see Lucy, poor gal, gooin' off her napper. Then one night I caught her wipin' her eyes and havin' a bit of a tune in the passage and she said it wur more'n flesh and blood could bear. Tupman and Olly and Gunner and Ponto wur all fer bouncing Pouchy out but I said—'

At this point my Uncle Silas suddenly broke off, looking uncommonly crafty, his bloodshot eye half-shut, the other reflectively contemplating a lump of well-burnt potato skin.

'Allus teks me back, whenever I git a-holt of a hot tater.' He laughed very softly, shaking his head. 'Never fergit it. See it now.'

My potato was cooler now and I sat eating the buttery salty flesh with relish too, waiting to hear what happened.

'I recollected seeing a chap once in a pub over at Swineshead. He wasn't quite all ninepence and two fellers put rum in his beer. Knock-out. Fast asleep in five minutes, just like a baby.'

Here I said that if this was all they did to Pouchy it sounded pleasant rather than otherwise and anyway harmless enough.

'Well, it ain't quite all,' Silas said and once again he laughed very softly, his lips shining red with wine, 'it ain't quite all. Fust we treated him to a beer wi' one rum in it, then one wi' two in it, then one wi' three in it. Lucy wur slippin' on 'em in and we wur a-keepin' Pouchy talking. He wur very happy and in about half hour or so he went out like a light.'

'And then?'

Before answering my Uncle Silas took a long swig of wine and laughed with all his old fruity wickedness.

'I went out and got a good big hot tater.'

And what, I begged him to tell me, did they do with the hot potato?

'Dropped it into his breeches.'

'Front or back?'

'Well, he wur a-sittin' down at the time, so we couldn't very well git it down the back.'

He laughed again, really loudly this time, and said he wisht I'd bin there. Had I ever heard a pig being killed? It sounded just like that.

'Injury permanent?' I said.

'Well, I don't know about that. But it wur a good big tater and we got it well down there.'

Now I noticed that he had finished his first potato

and I opened the oven door and took out another. As he pressed it with his thumb even he recoiled a bit and said blandly:

'Sting a tidy bit when they're hot, boy.'

As I sat watching him break the skin of the potato with his crusty fingers, I begged to know what happened to Pouchy after that.

'Well, it wur a funny thing. He sort of went downhill. Took to the beer very bad. Went to the dogs. Never boasted about women no more. And in the end he wur half a cripple.'

This, I said, didn't at all surprise me.

'That's right,' he said. Slowly he picked up the bottle of elderberry, filled up the two glasses, held his own up to me and gave me one of those long solemn blood-shot winks of his. 'Lost his pride. Onaccountable bad. Pass us the butter.'

The House by the River

'I think I've found a cottage. A house, rather. On the River Ouse. I mean right on it. The garden actually runs right down to the river bank and there's a quarter of a mile of fishing. It belongs to a lady who finds it too big for her and she wants to sell. Sounds marvellous, absolutely idyllic.'

'Have you seen it yet?'

'No. I just saw this advertisement in the county paper.'

'Never believe what you read about houses in advertisements.'

'Don't be cynical. The point is are you free this afternoon? If you are I'll come over and pick you up, and we'll run out and see it. All right? About three?'

The voice at the other end of the telephone was that of my friend Alex Sanderson. Alex was in the business of making boots and shoes and hated it. I had long had a suspicion that his ultimate dream in life was to live in the sort of house he had just described and grow tomatoes or strawberries or flowers and do a little fishing in the summer. Alex was unmarried and looked less like the businessman he was than a country solicitor or doctor or something of that sort. His features, especially his hands, were delicate. He suffered a good deal from catarrh. He wore spectacles and when he took them off, which he did frequently in order to polish them, his eyes had a curious distant diffidence which in turn gave him a look of painful hesitancy, as if he couldn't make up his mind about something. That in fact was a dominant characteristic of his and was precisely why he was fetching me in order to view his idyllic dream.

We drove out in leisurely fashion to the Valley of the Ouse. The July afternoon was exquisite. When we reached the crest of the valley we could see below us the broad curves of the river winding through tranquil meadows and on the surface of the water what at first looked like flotillas of white ducks but which were in fact pure shining white water-lilies.

'God, I love this bit of country,' Alex said. 'I've always felt I wanted to live here.'

I said that I loved it too. It was indeed idyllic.

'If my map reading is correct,' Alex said, 'it ought to be down the next turning on the left. That should take us to the river.'

We duly turned left, drove past a small labourer's cottage and eventually drew up at a rather big untidy-looking Edwardian house in red brick that truly stood, as the advertisement had said, on the bank of the river.

'This must be it,' Alex said. 'I'll give the bell a ring.'

I heard the jangle of the bell echoing through the house. It stopped at last and there was no answer. Alex rang again, and again there was no answer. Then Alex rang a third time and again the same thing happened. I don't know why, but the sound of that bell had an uncanny effect on me. There was something mournful, if not sinister, about its jangling echo.

Alex came back to the car. 'Doesn't seem to be anybody at home. I'll try round the back.'

Before Alex could turn I suddenly noticed a figure standing behind him. It hadn't been there a moment or two before and it suddenly seemed to have materialized out of nowhere.

Then Alex noticed it too. It was always a characteristic of his to be extremely polite and he at once raised his hat and said:

'Miss Waterfield? Good afternoon. My name is Sanderson.'

The figure didn't move and offered no word in answer. It was a very tall figure and very broad and angular, I thought, for a woman. It stood with feet wide apart and hands clasped behind its back. The features of the face were strong and bony and on the upper lip was a dark smear of incipient moustache.

'I wrote to you about the house.'

'Ah! yes. You wrote to me about the house.'

The voice was remarkably strong but it was not in fact the strength of the voice that impressed me or that the words sounded almost guttural. Like the sound of the bell echoing through the house it was the repetition of the words that had an uncanny, almost sinister effect on me.

'I hope it's convenient to look over the house.'

'I shall have to make it convenient.'

This remark struck through the very heart of the idyllic afternoon like a chill.

'Better come in.'

Alex said thank you and, turning to me, asked if I was coming too.

Suddenly I didn't want to go into that house and I was on the verge of saying so when Alex gave me a short, pleading look and said:

'Yes. You must. That's what I brought you for. I really want your opinion.'

If the air had been deliciously warm outside it struck uncommonly cold inside. Alex in fact gave a catarrhal cough or two as we entered the wide carpetless hall in which, I noticed, stood an umbrella stand full of walking sticks. As I noticed them I noticed too that Miss Waterfield gave me a look of strong suspicion and I got the impression that she had somehow taken a singular dislike to me.

I thought this was a good point at which to say that I had left my camera in the car and that I'd go back and fetch it. I duly did this. When I got back into the hall there was no sign of either Alex or Miss Waterfield but there was a strong smell of tobacco smoke in the air. I followed it through the hall, at the end of which a door leading to a long oak-panelled room was open. I heard the voices of Alex and Miss Waterfield coming from the room and I went in.

Miss Waterfield, again standing in her habitual attitude of legs wide apart and hands clasped behind her back, was puffing heavily at a pipe, blowing strong clouds of smoke.

'This is the sitting-room,' Alex said. 'Rather nice, I think. You like it?'

I didn't like it and I didn't answer. There was something stuffily impersonal about that room. It was heavy
with shadow. You often hear of houses needing a
woman's touch, a vase of flowers, pretty curtains and so
forth. But here there was no hint of a feminine touch nor
any hint of anything at all to relieve the unremitting
gloom.

'Miss Waterfield is going to show me the rooms upstairs. Will you come up too? I'd like it if you would.
Or perhaps we should have a look at the river first,
while it's fine. It feels a bit thundery to me.'

We walked to the river. Miss Waterfield took one
stride to two of mine and Alex's. The river was pretty
with white water-lilies, long skeins of emerald water
weed, yellow mimulus and blue water forget-me-not.
After walking a short distance I said I expected Alex
would like a picture of the house and he said yes, he
would.

I turned to point my camera at the house and immediately I was assailed by a strange impression. It
was that the house was watching us. And for some
curious reason I suddenly felt it was like another Miss
Waterfield, a tall, gaunt personification of her in red
brick. Then as I started to focus with the camera I got
another and this time more sinister impression. It was
that there was really a face, actually watching, from one
of the upstairs windows. It was gone in a second and I
was left with the chilly, uneasy notion that I had been
the victim of a mocking hallucination.

We walked farther up the river, coming presently to
a bend that provided a shallow, limpid pool. In the pool

were some dozens of fish, quite motionless except for occasional slight quivers of tails and fins, all silver and red in the afternoon sunshine.

'Roach,' I said.

'Rudd.'

No single word could have been more withering. It confirmed for me beyond all doubt that Miss Waterfield had conceived a deep fundamental dislike of me. I turned to Alex.

'If you and Miss Waterfield want to go upstairs to see the rest of the house please go ahead. I'll walk a little further along the river.'

'Oh! no, no. You must come. I really do value your opinion. Do come.'

There was always something touching about Alex's uncertainties. He could never really make up his own mind. If he discovered a new girl to take out to dinners or dances it was always essential that he introduce her to you. 'Do tell me what you think of her. Frankly I mean.' And for that reason, I suppose, he had never married.

We went back to the house. If Miss Waterfield's attitude to me had grown rapidly more chill and withering I now noticed that hers towards Alex had grown warmer. At one point she actually took his arm.

The stairs leading to the upper storeys of the house were exactly like the rooms below: shadowy and full of gloom. Miss Waterfield showed us into a large funereal bedroom in which I noticed, in one corner, a double-barrelled shotgun, several fishing rods, a shooting stick and a heavy riding crop.

'How many bedrooms are there?' Alex said.

'Five on this floor. But two I never use.'

'What about the next floor?'

'Don't need them. Always keep them locked.'

We looked at two more bedrooms, both complete with old-fashioned marble wash-stands and two brass bedsteads, one of which I felt had, with its thrown-back sheets, been recently slept in.

As we looked at them I felt all of Alex's uncertainties coming back. I felt that once again he was about to plead for my opinion and sure enough he did.

'Well, what do you think? How does it strike you?'

'Of course you'll have to have a proper survey.'

'Survey? Survey?' Miss Waterfield said. 'What survey?'

'It's customary to have a proper survey carried out by a competent person.'

'Not in this case. The property is structurally sound. It has always been kept in good repair. What purpose could a survey serve?'

'There are such things as dry rot. Faulty damp courses. Defective gutters. Drains not working properly—'

'Piffle.'

'Exteriors,' I said, 'don't necessarily reveal what is underneath.'

Miss Waterfield now gave me a glance of such deliberate hostility that it is no exaggeration to call it malicious. Indeed her eyes had in them an almost diabolical coldness as she suddenly thumped a large hand hard against the bedroom wall.

'Structurally sound, I tell you. Absolutely. Like a

fortress.' She turned to Alex. 'Perhaps you'd like to see the cellars? There may be further defects for your friend to discover? Come along.'

To my disturbed astonishment she actually put her arm round Alex's shoulder. I found the moment acutely embarrassing, so much so that when Alex again started to express his uncertainties I begged to be excused the visit to the cellars, saying that if Miss Waterfield had no objection I would like to take a picture of the river valley from the window at the end of the landing.

'Don't let me hinder you.'

Alex and Miss Waterfield went downstairs. I walked slowly to the window at the end of the landing. That exquisite pastoral scene of river, meadows, willows and water-lilies now seemed even more entrancing after the stifling claustrophobic gloom of the house and I stood for some minutes gazing down on it, thinking of Alex's words 'I love this bit of country' and my own brief reply 'I love it too.'

How long this reverie of admiration lasted I have now no idea. The silence of the house and the utter tranquillity of the world of river and meadows outside together produced such a deep sense of embalmment that I might have stood there for as long as twenty minutes or so. Another thing than the river, the meadows, the willows and the water-lilies that attracted my gaze was a column of smoke from a bonfire at the end of the garden. The air was so still that it rose, greyish-white, in true perpendicular, like some vaporous Indian rope-trick that might at any moment disappear into thin air.

I was still intent on watching this when I thought I

thought I heard a sound behind me. It sounded like the click of a door being either opened or shut. I turned and there at the other end of the corridor stood a man.

He was dressed in a brown velvet jacket, purple trousers and a green kerchief round his neck. He had blue feminine eyes and pale slender hands that he kept clasped together in front of him. For some moments he neither moved nor spoke. We simply gazed at each other. Then just as I was about to make some remark, partly of explanation, partly of apology for being there at all, he suddenly turned in silence, took a key from his pocket, opened the door of one of the rooms that Miss Water-field always kept locked and disappeared.

My old sense of chill came back and I went downstairs. Alex and Miss Waterfield were in the garden. Miss Waterfield was saying that she would confirm something by letter and Alex said to me:

'Well, did you get a good picture?'

My absorption in other things had been such that I hadn't in fact taken a picture. The only picture I had was one in my own mind.

'Well,' Miss Waterfield said, 'you will write to me when you get my letter. Or better still perhaps you would care to come and see me again.'

'I'd certainly like to do that.'

'Good. It's been very nice to see you.'

Alex said it had been nice to see her too and once again she put a hand across his shoulder, giving it an almost affectionate squeeze.

'Well, good-bye,' she said, 'if you'll excuse me I must go and look at my bonfire. I don't want it to go out. If you like you can go out along the river bank.'

She held out her hand and Alex took it. She held his for some long time and then let it go, I thought, with more than a little reluctance. I held out my own hand but once again she gave me that calculated stare of hostility and declined to take it.

Alex and I walked along the river bank. Some distance away we paused and turned to look back. Miss Waterfield was standing by her bonfire and once again the house, like some gaunt red-brick personification of her, seemed to be watching us.

Suddenly as we stood there the bonfire gave a great belch of smoke, completely enveloping her, so that it was as if the Indian snake trick had been performed.

'Well, I shall come to see her again.'

'Her?'

'Yes. Whatever makes you say that?'

'Him.'

While the incredulous astonishment on Alex's face was growing I stood thinking of the man upstairs.

'*Him?*' Alex said. 'You don't mean—'

'Exteriors,' I said, 'don't always reveal what is underneath.'

A stunned Alex had no answer and we stood for a few moments looking at the smoke of the bonfire rising to the blue July sky. There was no sign of anyone near.

'Suddenly seems to have disappeared completely,' Alex said.

'Let him go,' I said.

I took one last look at the house with its many windows that seemed to be staring down at us. Upstairs the window